Credits and Acknowledgements

The material in this book was inspired by the work of Marius Barbeau in *Haida Myths Illustrated by Argillite Carvings, Bulletin No. 127, Anthropological Series No. 32 p*ublished by the National Museum of Canada in 1953. Barbeau noticed similarities between Northwest Indian mythology and classic tales familiar to Europeans and Polynesians.

I am also grateful to Chief Henry Speck, Kwakiutl artist also known as Chief Ozistalis of the Tla-Wis-Tsis of Turnour Island and the other talented Haida artists I met while researching a series of articles on Northwest Indian art for *The Montreal Star* in 1964.

The stories are fictionalized versions of four of the Homeric legends depicted by Haida totem poles. They were written to entertain and the names of the characters have been created by the author and are not in the Haida language.

The illustrations are by artist Julia Lee Sadowski who sees the spirits in the cedar. The photographs on the cover and pages 2 and 3 are courtesy of the Library and Archives, Canada. Their website at (http://www.archivescanada.ca/english/index.html)
provides access to archival resources in more than 800 repositories across Canada. For more information, please visit the Sources and References section on Page 87.

To members of the Haida and all Northwest tribes: I hope you accept this work as a tribute to your magnificent heritage and a way to show that the basic values taught from generation to generation are common to all of us under this sun.

Eve Dumovich

Credit: Geological Survey of Canada Collection, Tribes _ Haida "Skedans Indian village, Haida tribe. Louise Island, Queen Charlotte Islands, British Columbia, Canada, July 18th, 1878, photographed by G.M. Dawson, Library and Archives Canada, accession number 1969-120, negative 248, reproduction copy number PA 37754

Index

The Spirit of Haida Gwaii: The Jade Canoe
Artist: Bill Reid, Haida, 1994

Originally conceived and created for the Canadian embassy in Washington D.C., the sculpture was first created in 1986 as a 1/6-scale clay maquette. The first bronze casting was completed in 1991 and donated to Her Majesty the Queen in Right of Canada (the Government of Canada) by Nabisco Brands Ltd., Toronto, Canada. It was put on display November 1991 at the embassy and titled *The Spirit of Haida Gwaii: The Black Canoe*. A second and final casting titled *The Spirit of Haida Gwaii, The Jade Canoe*, was commissioned by the Vancouver International Airport Authority in 1993. It was completed at the Tallix Foundry under the supervision of Bill Reid and installed at the airport on April 18, 1996.
Credit: *http://www.yvr.ca/en/about/art-architecture/Art-Haida-Gwaii.aspx*

Introduction

Haida have lived along the Pacific Northwest coast for more than ten thousand years. Where they came from is still a matter of discussion but in 1953, Canadian anthropologist, Marius Barbeau, published this version of the tribes' origin:

"Six canoe loads of people sailed out of the bitter seas, once long ago. They were on their way toward sunrise. Although they called themselves Fugitives, they were really seekers of a warmer climate and the Promised Land – the fabled Leesems or Temlaham.

"Famished and weary from a long peerless trek, they at last spied a wild wooded coast in the calm waters ahead. It looked unlike anything they had ever known and it happened to be Kodiak Island in Alaska, at the eastern end of the Aleutian Archipelago just south of the Bering Sea. There they set forth ashore and pitched their camp. Soon they met the savage folk of the grizzly bear tribe, made friends with them and found life to their liking. In time their camp swelled into a village under the leadership of Salmon Eater."

According to anthropologists, after settling in Alaska, some Haida tribes paddled their canoes south, looking for new fishing and hunting grounds. They established settlements along the North Coast of British Columbia, Canada, in what the European discoverers later called the Queen Charlotte Islands. June 3, 2010, the Haida Gwaii Reconciliation Act officially renamed the islands Haida Gwaii as part of the reconciliation protocol between British Columbia and the Haida people.

Haida families lived in lodges with totem poles at each supporting beam. The entrance was often through a tunnel through the base of a pole. Totems included the salmon, the halibut, the raven, the frog, the eagle, the bear, the killer whale, the crow, the thunderbird and various magical sea birds.

The poles told the stories that were passed from generation to generation and, as Barbeau noted in the preface to *Haida Myths Illustrated by Argillite Carvings,* many were similar to the classic legends from other ancient cultures.

"Although the myths and tales all belong to the Haida, they are not their monopoly. They form only a minor branch on a huge mythological tree which belongs to most of humanity. This cultural growth at first germinated and developed in the Old World – Asia and Europe; then, during the last millennia, it spread by oral transmission in migratory tribes to the New World at large, and then to the Haida on the Queen Charlotte Islands in the North Pacific, " Barbeau wrote.

The Haida developed a complex society on the islands, using cedar trees in many ways. The bark was woven into clothing and baskets and the wood used for masks, bentwood boxes, houses, totem poles and canoes. Their art reflected their belief that everything is connected." "Yahguudang" is the Haida word that means "respect for all living things." The Haida use of copper and their conical headgear are believed to have come from their Mongolian heritage. Copper was the ultimate symbol of wealth among the Haida and is associated with the mythological Copper Woman

The first documented contact between the Haida and Europeans was in 1774 when Juan Pérez, an 18th-century Spanish explorer became the first European to sight, examine, name and record the islands.

At that time, the Haida population was about 15,000. But by 1900, only 350 people remained. The rest were killed by smallpox, typhoid, measles and syphilis.

By 2014, there were about 4,000 Haida living in the Haida Gwaii that has two main islands: Graham Island in the north and Moresby Island in the south. Other major islands include Anthony, Langara, Louise, Lyell, Burnaby, and Kunghit Islands. With a total landmass of 3,931 square miles (10,180 square kilometers), it also includes 150 smaller islands.

Anthony Island and the island of Ninstints became a UNESCO World Heritage Site in 2006 and other islands are protected under federal legislation as Gwaii Haanas National Park Reserve.

The Haida Gwaii is separated from the British Columbia mainland to the east by Hecate Strait. Vancouver Island lies to the south, across Queen Charlotte Sound, while Alaska, U.S., is to the north, across the Dixon Entrance.

Let's travel through the Doorway...

The Odyssey from Loon to Eagle

Conn knew he was different. He saw shapes in the sea foam and laughed when he saw swallows diving.

His real parents drowned when he was a baby so he lived with his uncle, Kwakiyans, the wealthiest man in the village. His uncle's lodge was at the mouth of the best salmon river for miles around. Neighboring Haida tribes traded otter skins with Kwakiyans for the right to fish in the river. Kwakiyans traded the otter skins for copper dishes made by people from the inland villages.

Kwakiyans said a loon laughed when Conn was born and its spirit had made Conn into a dreamer and not a worker. He and his wife, Gitrawn, constantly criticized Conn and never praised him.

To get away from his aunt and uncle, Conn visited other lodges in the village where they were kinder to him and let him join their fire circles where they told the old tales, sang the old songs, carved cedar into the shapes of magical animals and played game.

When Conn's aunt and uncle called him useless and said he had no self-discipline, he felt sad because he didn't know how to change himself into somebody they might like.

One morning, Conn noticed that Kwakiyans was angrier than usual.

"I should have won that trade!" Kwakiyans shouted. "But, no, that fool in the Wolf lodge tricked me and kept the copper for himself. When I let him make the deal with the Inland Crows, he promised me he'd trade with me afterwards and I would get the copper. Then he changed his mind!"

Kwakiyans glared around the lodge as everybody backed into the shadows. He saw Conn standing by the fire, eating a breakfast cake.

"What are you staring at, you stupid boy?" Kwakiyans cried. "Get out of here! Find something to do that will help the family and that'll pay for your food!"

Conn ran outside, tears filling his eyes.

What can I do? he thought. Maybe I could make some arrows. Arrows are useful. Even Uncle Kwakiyans should like them.

Conn walked to the beach where the river joined the sea and squatted to examine the rocks. He selected the one he knew could be chipped into arrowhead.

As Conn worked, he listened to the wind in the trees. It seemed to tell him what to do. Conn selected cedar branches for the arrows' shafts and polished them until they gleamed. Then he wove a holder for the arrows out of soft cedar-root fibers and decorated it with seashells.

By the time he finished, a red sun had slipped behind the trees and the moon lit his way back to the lodge where Kwakiyans was in a better mood. His uncle had finished his dinner and was leaning against a wall smoking his pipe when Conn handed him the arrows in their container.

Kwakiyans didn't smile when he saw the gift but he did nod with a look that could have been approval.

"Well," Kwakiyans said. "You can be useful with your hands if you stick to making useful things. Your father could carve but he preferred making ornaments rather than tools. Your mother was a talented weaver. But, like you, she spent too much time laughing and not enough time working."

Conn looked at his uncle with interest. This was new. Maybe the arrows had worked. Kwakiyans had never told him anything about his real parents and he had always been afraid to ask. Now Kwakiyans seemed more talkative.

"Was my father from this village?" Conn asked carefully.

His uncle shook his head.

"My sister met your father at a gathering of the Eagle tribe. Even though his family was poorest in the lodge, she fell in love and married him. She thought she could pay their expenses by weaving spruce-bark blankets."

"What happened to them?" Conn asked.

Kwakiyans snorted.

"They both drowned when you were a baby. Your father was as bad at business as he was good at avoiding work. He traded some of his finest work for a leaky canoe. He took your mother for a ride in it and they never came back. Lucky for you, they had left you with us. So we kept you."

Conn was not sure he felt all that lucky.

Kwakiyans, yawned, stood up, took the arrows and left for is sleeping area.

Conn stretched out before the fire, stared into the flames and tried to imagine his mother and father. They sounded like nice people. He wished they were still alive. He couldn't remember their faces.

"There you are! Doing nothing again!"

The shrill voice of his aunt, Gitrawn, broke into his thoughts. Conn looked up at her red face and her yelling mouth. His sadness turned to irritation.

"You have a mosquito on your forehead," Conn said. There was no mosquito but Conn wanted to bother his aunt. He knew she hated mosquitoes.

Gitrawn slapped her forehead hard. Conn giggled.

"You get out of here! Just leave!" Gitrawn shouted. "You don't do anything except fish and whittle and eat our supplies! Get out! Spend the night in the cold! Don't come back without something useful!"

Conn's throat tightened and his eyes burned. He jumped to his feet, ran through the doorway and down to the river. Nothing he did made any difference, he thought miserably as he reached the shadowy bank. In the moonlight, the water was purple. A cold wind blew black slivers of clouds across the moon.

Silver shapes rippled across the river. Conn wondered if those were the water spirits rising to the surface. Cedar and hemlock trees along the bank speared the sky. Conn heard an owl hoot in the distance and the rustling of night animals as they crept across the river to drink. Conn picked handfuls of red huckleberries from a nearby bush. Once his stomach was full, he used his stone chisel to cut some cedar branches to cover himself as he lay down between the tree's roots. The soft ground was thick with needles. The roots protected him from the wind and gave him a place to rest his head. Conn fell asleep to the sound of waves lapping the gravel bank.

As the night paused between dark and dawn, Conn sat up. What had wakened him? Then he heard it again. A loon was laughing. The sound echoed eerily over the black river.

The Loon

Conn shivered. He knew the spirits gathered during that moment before the sun wakes. The night spirits rest, having done their work. The clouds do not move. The sky is neither dark nor light. The earth stirs slowly as the day spirits move reluctantly into action. The frogs stir and birds lift their sheltering feathers.

The loon's laugh shattered the silence a second time. Conn stared at the water. It rippled with strange shadows.

Again the loon laughed and the shadows took form. He saw an almost transparent canoe with two passengers. He knew they were the ghosts of his mother and father. As he watched, the shapes of his parents changed. One became a loon with a spot of scarlet on her throat. The other became an eagle with pure white head and tail. For a moment, Conn saw them very clearly. Then, the canoe disappeared into the black and silver waves. The loon and the eagle flew away and dissolved into purple clouds rising above the mist.

Conn blinked. That instant, dawn broke. The sky grew pink. The shapes and shadows had the comforting solidness of daytime things. They were not dreams but real rocks, trees and logs, colored by the brightening sky.

Then, a real loon swam across the river. It was the largest bird Conn had ever seen. Its back and side were the dark gray of the dawn waters. Its neck was a little lighter, and its throat was the color of the rising sun.

"How beautiful you are!" Conn cried.

The loon swam slowly to shore. Conn ran to the water's edge and sat with his feet hanging over the bank. The loon swam closer and nuzzled his knees with its beak. Conn stroked its feathers. The loon looked up at Conn and seemed to sigh. It climbed onto the bank and lay down, placed its head in Conn's lap – and died.

Conn was overcome with grief; his eyes filled with tears and a lump grew in his throat. He knew the loon had been his friend. Perhaps it had held the spirit of his mother. Now it, too, was dead.

He looked down at the creature. "Nobody will see your beautiful feathers anymore," Conn said sadly. Then he remembered how he could keep the spirit of the loon with him forever. Perhaps it had come to him for that reason.

With great care and respect, he skinned the loon so that its feathers remained intact. He spread the skin to dry on a rock as he prepared soft thread from the inner bark of the cedar tree.

Conn worked all day and far into the night. When he had finished, he had made a magnificent cloak from the loon. The hood and the back were dark gray; the front was light gray. The bright red fathers lay at his throat. The beak was a visor on the hood.

Conn put on the finished cloak and looked at his reflection in the river.

"I look just like that giant loon," he thought happily. Then, he went to sleep in his cedar root bed, warmed by his magical cloak.

He woke the next morning to shouts and laughter from the river. Peeping from behind the tree, he saw some of his cousins fishing from a canoe.

"Where is that lazy Conn?" he heard one of them ask.

"Oh, he is off somewhere, loafing as usual," said someone else.

Conn, still wearing his loon cloak, dove into the water. Like all the young boys in his village, he was an excellent swimmer. The loon's feathers skimmed through the water. He swam underwater until he saw the bow of his cousin's canoe. Then he surfaced.

"Ahaw! Ahaw! Ahaw!" he cried, giving a perfect imitation of a loon. Then he dove again.

"A giant loon!" cried his frightened cousins. "That's a bad sign!"

Conn surfaced again. "Ahaw! Ahaw! Ahaw!" he cried.

His cousins were so terrified that they paddled only on the side of the canoe furthest from Conn and leaned the wrong way. The canoe tipped over and they all fell into the water.

Conn swam underwater back to shore. Laughing, he went back into his cedar shelter. Then he threw the cloak over his arm and walked back to his uncle's house.

Inside, his aunt, Gitrawn, was weaving a blanket out of softened cedar strands. The men were out hunting, fishing or trading. Only the fire pit nearest his aunt provided light and heat. The rest of the building was cold and dark.

Conn moved quietly past the sleeping platforms and storage areas toward his aunt. She looked up from her work.

"Oh. It's you," Gitrawn said grumpily.

"I am sorry I played a trick on you," Conn said. "I just couldn't help it. I will try to do better. I want you to like me."

"Huh," his aunt replied. "You never do anything useful. How could anybody like you? You're too lazy. I bet you didn't bring anything useful back with you."

Conn smiled. "I brought a beautiful cloak," he said. "I made it myself. It keeps the rain and cold away."

His aunt looked at the loon cloak. Its colors gleamed in the firelight.

"Feathers!" she snorted. "What's wrong with the usual kind of cloak? You are just like your father used to be, always thinking of something that's more decorative than useful."

Conn turned away sadly. He had hoped his aunt would be proud of the beautiful work he had done.

Then he noticed that one of the feathers was loose. He plucked it off and threw it into the fire.

Woosh! It blazed with the brightness of the sun, and the whole room was filled with light.

Conn's aunt was so frightened that she jumped up, tripped on her loom and fell over, landing on her back with her feet straight up in the air.

Conn was still laughing when his uncle came through the doorway. Gitrawn jumped to her feet and cried: "He did that on purpose! He knew that loon feather was explosive!"

Kwakiyans grabbed Conn's shoulders and shook him.

"How dare you!" he shouted. "You're an ungrateful fool!"

With that, Kwakiyans grabbed Conn and shoved him out the door.

"You'll sleep outside tonight again, like the lowest of our dogs!" Kwakiyans cried. "Then we'll see what we'll do with you!"

Conn spent the night huddling against the outside wall. The loon cloak kept him warm but did not keep him from being sad. He thought of running away forever but he was afraid that his uncle would catch him and make his punishment even worse.

"I'd better stay here and take what is coming to me," he told himself.

The next morning Kwakiyans came out of the house and shouted:

"Come here, Conn!"

Conn hurried to stand in front of his uncle, afraid of what lay ahead.

"We are going sea otter hunting," Kwakiyans said. "You will sit in the front of the canoe to keep watch."

Conn wondered when he would be punished. A hunting trip was hard work but not really a punishment. Kwakiyans didn't say anything else but strode toward the riverbank. Conn followed and, still carrying his cloak, kneeled where he was told, in the front of the one of the long, carefully carved canoes. The river was calm and the sun was hot.

The Haida paddled their canoes out of the river's mouth and into the dark blue sea. The canoes rose easily over the surf and were soon skimming gently across the foam-tipped waves. Once the sun had burned away the morning mists, the water glistened as if it was sprinkled with diamonds. Sea gulls wheeled overhead. There was not a cloud in the sky. Conn leaned his head against the prow and sighed happily. Perhaps he wouldn't be punished after all.

The even beat of the Haida paddles made Conn drowsy. He dozed off.

"Wake up!" Kwakiyans cried. "You are useless even as a lookout! Well! You'll pay for it now!"

The chief signaled to all the canoes to come close to each other. Kwakiyans looked at Conn and said angrily: "A few hours in this sun will teach you a lesson you'll never forget!"

Kwakiyans ordered all of his men out of Conn's canoe and into the other boats. They took their paddles with them.

"So long, dreamer!" Kwakiyans cried. He and his men paddled away. Conn was left alone in a canoe, floating free on the wide and salty sea.

Conn tried to get the middle of the canoe so that he could paddle with his hands but found he could not move. His uncle had spread spruce gum on the floor of the canoe, knowing that Conn would become stuck as he kneeled in the bow.

The sun's hot rays burned Conn's head. He wanted to cry. He believed his uncle had decided he was too useless to live and wanted him to die at sea. The brightness of the water began to hurt his eyes. He struggled to pull his loon cloak over his head. In its shade, he began to feel better.

Very carefully Conn managed to lean the canoe to one side just enough so that the hot sun softened the spruce gum. He got one leg free. He leaned the other way and soon his other leg was free. Careful to avoid any more spruce gum, Conn moved to the center of the canoe.

Shielded from the sun by his cloak, Conn pushed through the water with his hands. It was slow going and he needed a drink of water.

"I'll never make it home," he thought miserably. "My uncle never meant me to come back." A lump came to his throat and tears burned his eyes.

A small breeze rippled the burning blue water and the loon feathers rustled gently.

Conn had an idea. He turned his cloak upside down and spread spruce gum from the floor of the canoe on the hood of the cloak. He put his feet inside the hood and then stood up, careful not to fall overboard. He spread the hem apart with his hands raised high above his head. The spruce gum kept the cloak and Conn's feet securely fastened to the bottom of the canoe. The wind caught the cloak and blew it out behind his head like a balloon. The canoe began to slide swiftly across the water with the loon cloak acting as a sail and Conn himself as the mast. The wind blew Conn in his cloak all the way to shore.

The canoe ran aground on the pebbled beach and Conn put down his arms. They were stiff and sore. His throat was dry. He spread the cloak in the sun until its heat softened the gum again and he could detach it from the boat. Then he folded the cloak under his arm and stumbled up the beach to a fresh-water creek that bubbled into the sea. He scooped the water to his face, drank and cooled himself down.

Exhausted, he went deeper into the forest, found a soft spot under a tree, wrapped himself in the cloak and fell asleep.

That evening, as usual, back at Kwakiyans' house, Conn's aunt and the other women set out carved bowls filled with fish oil, berry and sorrel cakes and sweet pine bark. They put red-hot rocks in water contained by a wooden box and poached a fresh-caught salmon.

The family members, tired from a busy day, gathered on their sleeping platforms to wait for the meal to begin.

Kwakiyans crouched by the fire and watched Gitrawn cook.

"We did it," he told her happily. "We finally got rid of the boy. I don't think he'll be back."

"One less mouth to feed," Gitrawn replied.

Just then, Conn entered the doorway and stood in the shadows. Nobody saw him.

"I hate useless people," Kwakiyans continued. "Conn and his parents were completely useless. That boy's father was such a fool that he never realized the canoe I sold him was full of holes. He was so trusting!"

Kwakiyans laughed. Gitrawn cackled.

"And that woman of his was also a fool," Gitrawn snorted. "She claimed she could talk to birds!"

Conn gasped. He strode to the fireside and glared at his aunt and uncle.

Kwakiyans grunted: "So. You are back."

"I'm back and I heard you!" Conn shouted. "You call yourself a great chief but you are just a bad man! You sold my father a leaky canoe even though you knew that he could drown if he took it to sea!"

"Business is business," Kwakiyans said.

"Then you tried to get rid of me by leaving me in a canoe that you covered with sticky gum. You meant me to die of thirst!"

"Well you didn't," Kwakiyans said calmly. "I had faith you would survive if you really wanted to."

Conn clenched his fists.

"You and my aunt are both bad people! You may be good traders and powerful but you're mean and small in spirit!"

Kwakiyans jumped to his feet. "You're talking to a chief! he roared. "You're being disrespectful! You're banished forever from this house AND this village! Get out and never come back!"

Kwakiyans sons took out their knives and stood up. They gathered behind Kwakiyans with their blades pointed at Conn.

"Get out!" the oldest son shouted. "You must leave forever! The chief must always be respected!"

Conn looked around the room and did not see a sympathetic face. He ducked his head and ran out of the house. He knew he could never come back again.

Tears blinded him as he stumbled toward the sea. Once by the beach, he turned north and ran along the rocks as darkness fell. Huge drift logs blocked his way but he climbed over them and kept going. He had to get as far away as he could from the village he had once called home.

A few stretches of white sand separated the logs and rocks. Sand and sea birds hopped and fluttered at the low tide line, looking for insects. A sea gull dropped a mussel onto a rock where it broke. The gull gobbled up the sweet meat inside. Conn was hungry too but he did not want to stop.

Daylight faded and Conn thought the foaming surf looked like silver fur on a purple velvet cape. The sky was clear and the moon was full and bright. Conn decided to keep going as long as the moon gave him light. As he traveled, he thought about his lonely life in his uncle's house. He stroked the soft feathers of his cloak and felt better.

He saw moonlight gleaming off the sharp fins of killer waves circling in the deep water. Conn kicked a barnacle-covered rock like a ball ahead of him.

On and on he walked. Hours passed. Then the moon fell into the sea and the world prepared for dawn. Mists floated over the waves and silver. On and on he walked. Hours passed. Then the moon fell into the sea sand. Once again, Conn saw strange shapes in the water and on the beach around him. The dark drift logs looked like weird monsters with a life of their own. Ghostly canoes shimmered and disappeared. Giant kelp writhed like serpents in the shifting light.

A New Family

As the sky turned mauve, Conn looked inland and gasped. Above the trees he saw the tops of totem poles. He followed the trail of cedar bark between gnarled wind-bent trees into the forest until he reached the lodge. The poles at each corner were carved and colorful and the entrance was studded with shells. Smoke drifted into the dawn's fog through several holes in the roof

Conn didn't know where he was.

"I must have walked farther than I thought," he muttered. "Maybe I can get something to eat here."

As he approached the doorway, a girl about his age came out with a cedar bucket for water.

"Hello," she said. "Where did you come from?"

Conn decided to tell her the truth. That way he had nothing to hide and she would either accept him right away or reject him. If she didn't want him around, he would just move on.

"I'm Kwakiyans' nephew, Conn," he said. "Kwakiyans and his family told me to leave because I didn't show the chief enough respect."

To his relief, she threw back her head and laughed.

"My father doesn't really respect Kwakiyans either. Come, help me get water. Then you can come in for breakfast."

Conn's stomach was already rumbling with hunger. Her offer sounded wonderful.

"What's your name?" he asked as they walked to the creek nearby.

"My name is Hallate," she said.

Conn was nervous when he followed her into her home where family members surrounded the fire and the smaller children were already sucking on sticky berry cakes.

"This is Conn, Chief Kwakiyan's nephew," Hallate said. "He's joining us for breakfast."

"This is my father, Narnor, and my mother, Kanata," Hallate told Conn.

Narnor, beckoned to Conn to sit beside him. Conn gulped. He felt as if Hallate's father could read his mind.

Narnor's face looked like the sharp side of the distant mountain. His eyes were as gray as the winter sea. He wore a cloak that billowed with white feathers and his voice rumbled like the deepest places of a bubbling river.

"Your spirit is not like that of your uncle's," Narnor said. "It is larger and the color of dawn."

Conn knew then that Narnor was able to see the aura of a person's spirit. He had heard about this gift although Kwakiyans called it garbage because he did not believe in anything that could not be touched or sold.

"My uncle has told me to leave his lodge," Conn said sadly.

Kanata passed Conn a bowl of steamed fish.

Narnor smiled kindly. "You have a new home here," he told Conn. "This was meant to be. You have much to learn. But I think you'll learn what you need and learn it well."

Conn felt as if a warm breeze had blown through him.

"Today you will rest," Narnor said. "Tomorrow, you'll join us in our lives."

So Conn began his new time of growing, and for the next few years he learned about rocks, trees, the creatures of air, earth and water. He wore his loon cloak and it seemed to grow with him.

Narnor's family sang songs, told jokes and stories and made beautiful ornaments. Conn learned to laugh without feeling ashamed.

Hallate grew up with him and, one day, Conn saw her standing against the sea and realized that he loved her. She was more beautiful than the rising sun and he wanted to be with her forever. At the same time, he noticed that her eyes grew soft when she looked at him. Perhaps she felt the same way about him.

So in early summer as they walked beside the creek on a day so sunny that the water glittered with diamonds, Conn stopped, turned Hallate towards him put his arms on her shoulders and looked down at her.

"You're my friend and the most important person in my life," he said. "I'd like you to become my wife so that we could be together until it's time to go to the spirit world."

Hallate smiled up at him and blushed with happiness.

"I'd like that too," she said. "But my father must give his permission. "Not only that, but he will test you to see if you are strong enough. That is our tradition."

"Strong enough for what?" Conn was slightly offended. He knew he was in excellent shape.

"My father says that to marry, a person must be as strong as the wind and as soft as a tree. He'll give you a series of tasks to finish and when you finish them he'll know that you're right for me. "

"And if I don't?"

"You'll do fine. I know the spirits are on our side and each task will help you get ready for the years ahead."

Hallate moved away from him then and walked back towards the lodge.

That evening after dinner, Conn asked Narnor if he could speak to him alone. The two men walked through the totem to the outside where the moon was a silver sliver and wisps of dark clouds drifted across her surface.

"What you want to ask me about?" Narnor asked.

"I'd like your permission to marry Hallate," Conn said.

Narnor stared into Conn's eyes and Conn thought the old man was reading his soul.

"Did Hallate tell you what I would ask you to do?"

"She said you will give me a series of tasks that I must complete before you give your permission. But I am in very good shape and I believe I can do whatever you ask."

Narnor nodded approvingly.

"Good," he said. "For your first task, you will have to conquer the giant octopus."

Conn gasped. The octopus lived in a deep sea pool and he had heard of its great size. It was evil and dangerous and had killed many Haida. They said it had been made in the darkness where there are no good spirits and it was the family's most dangerous enemy.

"I will do that," he said with much more confidence than he felt.

"What can I do?" he asked Hallate later. "It could destroy me!"

"Out-think it," she told him. "My father would never ask you to do something you cannot do. Be smarter than the octopus."

The Octopus

Credit: *From catalog for Kwakiutl Art by Chief Henry Speck, published March, 1964, Vancouver Canada. "He was an inhabitant of the Under-Sea world. Some legends recounted his role as a warrior there. If a young man wished to gain supernatural power from underwater, he might wait for the Octopus to conduct him down."*

The next morning, Conn headed for the beach.

"I'll trap it," he decided.

Conn searched and found a strand of seaweed tough enough for his purposes. He used shredded spruce bark to turn the seaweed into a strong fishing line. With his knife, he carved a hook out of cedar wood and designed the hook so that when the octopus took the bait, a small piece of wood would float to the surface to show Conn he had caught his prey.

When the hook was finished, Conn wondered what he could use as bait. He decided to carve a giant salmon out of silver driftwood. It had to be big enough to attract the great octopus. Driftwood was heavy and would sink to the bottom.

The finished wooden salmon was in three pieces, connected by a strong strand of rope made from the root of a cedar tree. He made its scales from the glittering inner parts of mussel shells and fastened the scales to the wood with spruce gum.

Conn wound one end of the line around a nearby tree and tied it tightly. He attached the other end to the hook, baited the hook with his wooden salmon and threw the hook into the deepest part of the pool.

"That should hold the biggest beast," he told himself.

Then Conn sat on the shore and waited. It was a beautiful blue-sky day. The sun made the water clear and green for many feet down. The deepest part of the pool was black as night. Conn could see his line snaking downward into the darkness.

Suddenly, the wooden signal bobbed to the surface. Something had taken the bait!

"Aha!" Conn cried. He jumped to his feet , waving his knife in the air.

The water churned and frothed. A hideous gray limb, dripping with black slime, rose out of the water. It came toward Conn. Each of its suckers was as big as Conn's head.

"Yikes!" Conn cried. "I hope my line is strong enough!"

The seaweed and spruce bark line pulled and stretched. The tree to which the line was fastened bent double but Conn but the line held.

The water bubbled and spat white foam. Another hideous limb rose from the pool. It soared into the air and down toward Conn. He hacked it off with his knife and it fell to the ground, writhing and oozing black goo.

Again and again, the awful tentacles came from the sea and again and again, Conn slashed them to the ground. As he fought for his life, he thought of how fast the eagle dove after its prey and how its beak was so ready and so quick to grab its enemy. His arm became like the eagle's beak.

When he thought he could fight no more, the body of the octopus rose from the sea like a mountain of red, quivering flesh. It was almost as tall as the trees. Its eyes glared with the blackness of pure evil. It rose higher and higher on its remaining tentacles and then bent over Conn. Its beak was jagged and the brown green color of a swamp.

Conn ran forward to meet it. Just as the beak descended to attack him, he swerved to one side and stabbed the octopus in its black and horrible eye. He drove deep and the octopus fell dead at his feet.

Conn collapsed on the beach, exhausted.

He woke up to the sound of singing. Hallate and her father were leading a procession down the beach toward him. As they walked, the whole Haida family was singing about Conn and the strength the spirits had given him to destroy the evil octopus.

That evening, Narnor asked Conn to follow him outside the lodge where a half-moon silvered the ground; Conn asked Narnor again if he could marry Hallate.

He expected Narnor to agree. But the old man shook his head.

"I wish I could," Narnor said. "But last night, a spirit came to me in my dream. It told me you have yet to learn the freedom of the whale, the strength of the giant clam and the power of the eagle."

Conn's heart sank. Then he remembered what Hallate had said:

"My father will never ask you to do anything you cannot do."

Conn looked at Narnor. "What's my next mission?" he asked.

Narnor smiled at Conn.

"When the moon shows her full face again, you'll meet the whale."

For the next several evenings, Conn went outside and stared at the sky. Each night, the moon grew larger and larger. He saw the face of the moon as she grew. She had large eyes, a firm chin and firm lips. As she grew, it seemed to Conn that she was turning her head toward the earth and smiling down. Finally, she was almost completely facing hi.

That night Narnor called Conn to his side after the evening fire.

"Tomorrow, you and my men will take my strongest canoes and paddle beyond the sea foam. You, alone, will wait until the Great Whale visits you."

Conn gasped.

"I know about the Great Whale! He can destroy boats. Fishermen have drowned after seeing him!"

Narnor nodded sadly. "There are many who travel the seas before they have been blessed by the Great Whale's spirit. You must earn this blessing or you'll not return either."

Conn was really frightened. He had never been on a whale hunt. He didn't know the first thing about it.

"But..." he said.

"You must prove that you are man enough to marry Hallate," Narnor said firmly. "Enough talk."

When Conn told Hallate what her father had said, she sighed, afraid for Conn's life.

The Whale

As dawn turned the foaming sea gold, the men climbed into canoes and the women sang the song of the whale. The wind blew cold. Conn put on his loon cloak.

Narnor smiled at him. "T hat cloak will be your armor. The spirit of the loon will be your guide."

Conn forced himself to smile back, despite his fear.

The men paddled the canoes for several hours, going further and further from shore. The sun rose high, the sky was blue and the sea glittered around them like rippling silver. Suddenly, at the edge of the horizon where the sea met the sky, a white plume of water rose to the sun. It looked like a giant white feather bursting into space.

"There he is!" the men cried, and turned their canoes toward the plume. As they drew closer, Conn gasped. A whale as big as an island humped above the churning sea. The men sat quietly in their canoes. They did not reach for their spears or their arrows. They were perfectly still.

"What are we waiting for?" he asked.

The man closest to Conn said, "We are waiting for a sign from the Great Whale. Sometimes he has a gift for us."

"A gift?"

"The whales choose one of their own to come to us and give us their spirit. We do not know why. But every so often, one will sacrifice himself to us."

"Sacrifice?"

"All creatures are one. Sometimes we need each other. The whales know this and choose their own to give us oil and food. We can only take what they give and only when they come to us. And, sometimes, they choose one of us to take our spirit to join them in the depth of the seas. Our Chief Narnor says you will be chosen this day."

Conn understood and trembled.

Perhaps he would never go back to land, he thought. He would never see Hallate again. His spirit would be in the sea with the whales.

Then he thought, if that was what the whales wanted, he would join them in the mist. Perhaps he would see his mother and father again and would swim with their spirits.

The whale turned to face them. Conn saw the tiny glittering eyes in the huge black cliff that was the whale's head. Suddenly, it turned around and dove. Its tail rose above the bubbling water like a giant "Y".

The tail towered high and slapped down. A silver wave curled up and out of the deep, wrapped itself around Conn and dragged him from the canoe.

"Why?" he asked himself as he felt himself go under. He held his breath as long as he could because he knew that once he breathed in the sea, he would be lost from land forever. Deeper and deeper he went. The head of his loon cloak slipped over his face as he sank, and he could see nothing but pitch black.

Then, just about the time he thought he would burst from holding his breath, it occurred to him that his eyes did not sting as they should in sea water. He opened his mouth. No water entered it. The loon cloak's hood had become a type of diving helmet, trapping air inside.

Conn took a careful breath, then another. He was breathing! He felt himself start to float upward. After a while, he ran out of air inside the loon's hood. He pulled it from his head and held his breath again. Above him, the surface of the sea was a bright green emerald. Below him, huge dark shapes swam in circles. A mother whale and her baby floated in the darkness below his feet.

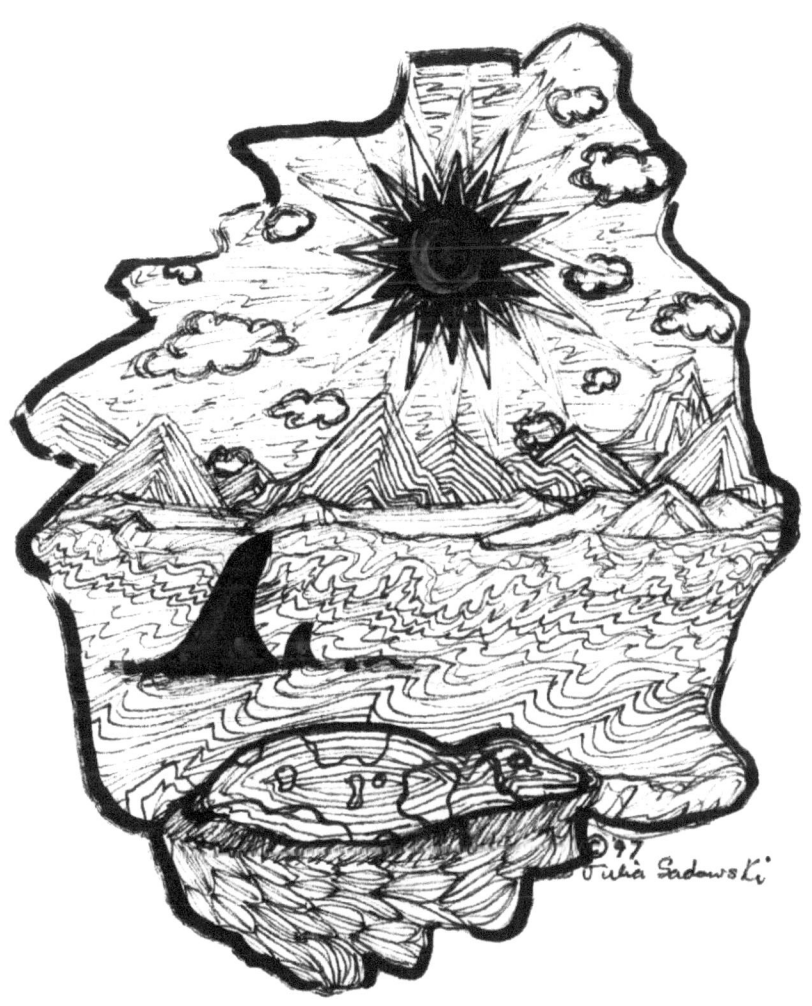

A new feeling seemed to come from them and he was filled with a great love for the baby whale. His eyes stung then, but not from sea water but with tears of love as he swam to the light.

His head burst from the water into the bright sun and red circles danced before his eyes. When the spots cleared, he could see great gray stretches of water, flat from sky to sky with no sign of land.

I must swim, he thought. They have released me to swim home but it is a very long way. He felt something solid under his body. The mother whale had come to the surface, her baby alongside and Conn found himself spread across the gentle giant's back.

The wind ruffled his hair and the feathers of his cloak as the mother whale swam to shore over the rounded waves, her baby bouncing beside her.

The air sparkled in his nose, the sun brightened his eyes and his spirits rose with every loop over the shining water. He was happier than he could have ever remembered.

This is how a mother's love feels, he told himself. How lucky I am to have finally learned what it is.

The shoreline was soon ahead, riding like a dark fringe on white waves. When the trees stood clearly on the horizon, the whale turned her head as if to say goodbye and then dove into the deep.

Conn was alone, swimming slowly and sadly toward the sandy beach.

The Giant Clam

He was only a mile from his destination when he felt a sharp pain in his ankle. He looked through the water and cried out, almost sounding sound like a loon.

A giant clam was clamped around his ankle. The pain was more than he could endure. The giant clam was going to drag him down and drown him within sight of land.

He cried out again and again. Once more tears stung his eyes but these were from pain and grief.

He was pulled down and he fought with all his might to get to the surface. The loon cloak billowed out and helped him stay afloat. But it gave way against the pulling of the clam. The loon cloak pulled from his shoulders as Conn was dragged to the dark rocks and caves where kelp strands tangled up in the cape's feathers. It broke from his shoulders as Conn struggled to the surface.

The Eagle

Conn battled to the surface but was pulled down a second time. He fought to the surface again.

Giant wings blocked the sun. Orange claws dangled above his head and black and white feathers stretched as far as he could see. The claws curled around his back and as the giant wings beat skyward Conn felt himself being lifted above the water. But the giant clam still held fast to his ankle.

The eagle bent its snow-white head and its golden eye flashed fire. The fire-red beak slashed at the clam dangling from Conn's foot. With a pop, the clam let go and splashed back into the sea.

Conn's ankle still throbbed with pain but he knew he had been saved. He looked up at the belly of the eagle as it carried him to shore. The eagle is made of clouds and fire, he thought. It is a powerful and good spirit.

The eagle flew to the rocky beach near the lodge and dropped Conn onto the warm pebbles. The sun had not yet set and the eagle beat its wings as it headed skyward again. Conn thought he saw joy in the golden eyes.

Conn got up and limped to the lodge. Inside, Hallate hugged him happily and Narnor ordered everyone to prepare a huge feast in honor of his victorious return.

That evening, Conn told the story of his adventures as the tribe clustered around the fire and the children ate sweet, dried-berry cakes.

As soon as Conn finished his story, Narnor stood up and went to a corner of a storage platform. He brought Conn a large cedar box. The box was decorated with carvings of eagles in flight.

"This box is filled with eagle feathers that have fallen to land," Narnor said, "You will make a cloak from these."

He paused and smiled. "You will wear the eagle cloak when you marry Hallate."

"Yes!" Conn cried.

During the next few weeks, while Hallate and the women planned the wedding, Conn wove a new cloak with a pure white hood and dark gray back. He carved a beak out of orange cedar for the helmet and its visor. It was finished by sunset the day before his wedding.

He tried it on and looked at his reflection in a tide pool. In the orange light, he looked like an eagle perched against the fading sun.

The power of the eagle, the strength of the clam and the serenity of whale mingled with the laughter of the loon in his heart. Conn knew he was ready to live a strong and good life.

Hallate and Conn were married in a glorious ceremony. Many new songs were written and many new dances performed.

Conn's totems were very powerful. In time, he took over as chief of Narnor's family. It is also said that Conn's Uncle Kwakiyans finally cheated so many people out of copper; they refused to do business with him. Kwakiyans lost his land and his house, and Conn, now chief of the Eagle totem, took it over.

Conn was forgiving and generous. He allowed Kwakiyans and Gitrawn to live in their own home until they left the earth. But his aunt and uncle never forgot that they were in debt to him so were angry and unhappy for the rest of their lives.

The Volcano Woman and the Weeping Totem

The Weeping Totem Pole of Tanu was as gray as the clouds that rode the skies. Visitors stared at it feeling its sadness. The pole, carved from a single tree, was in the shape of a man holding a frog.

Tears streamed from each of the man's eyes and each stream ended in the carving of a small boy. The base of the totem was the face of another large frog.

Another pole at the Haida village of Cumshewa was of an old grandfather in tears. It also had the faces of two little boys carved at the end of each stream of tears.

The totems show the sadness of a grandfather who was once known as Chief Always-Laughs.

Chief Always-Laughs was the leader of several Haida families near the Nass River. He spoke to the spirits of the animals and knew which ones were willing to share their spirits with the Haida and those that should be left alone.

"Never kill an animal just for fun," Chief Always-Laughs told his family.

"Never kill for sport. The Great Spirit has placed many living things in the water, on the land, and in the sea. We learn how to live with each other. The plants will cure our sickness, and feed us, if we will tend them and respect them as they grow. The animals, fish and birds will give us clothing, shelter and food, if we respect them as they grow.

"There is work for all life and we must love all living things. The Great Spirit will take care of us as long as we know our place in this world and honor the life around us. If we abuse the life around us, we will be punished."

Chief Always-Laughs made that speech at the evening fire again and again. It was important to him. Of course, after a while, people stopped listening to it; they had heard it too often. By the time his two grandsons, Ayuk and Gat, were old enough to go fishing they had heard his warning so often that as soon as he started to talk about the Great Spirit – they went to sleep,

Ayuk was 13 and the older of the two boys. He was tall for his age and loved to sing and dance. Chief Always-Laughs encouraged him to learn the words and notes of the ceremonial songs and showed him how to dance the ceremonial dances.

"The singing wind and the dancing fir tree are strong in Ayuk's heart," Chief Always-Laughs said proudly.

Gat was two years younger than Ayuk and a little shorter. Gat wanted to make canoes when he grew up so he spent many hours carving shapes in cedar and learning his craft.

Gat had a special talent for selecting the best tree for a canoe. He often led older members of the tribe into the forest to a perfect cedar. When the tree was cut down, Gat and the others hollowed out its center and dragged it to the edge of the river. They made the canoe's wood as smooth as silk with an adze.

Once the canoe shape was carved from the tree, the canoe-makers built fires around the carved tree and poured buckets of water into its hollowed-out center. They dropped red-hot rocks into the water and trapped the steam with heavy cedar mats. In time, the steam softened the hard cedar. The canoe-makers grabbed each side of the hollowed out tree and pulled. They pulled until the canoe popped into its right shape, with rounded sides and space inside for strips of cedar that would brace the sides and bottom.

The bow and the stern of the canoe were decorated with beautiful carvings and the tribe launched each canoe with a special ceremony, during which Ayuk danced and sang.

"You waste your time," Gat told his brother. "My canoes help the whole tribe. Your dances just entertain. With your strength, you could be a fine canoe carver!"

Ayuk smiled calmly, although he was angry.

"I'll leave that business up to you," he said. "My dances will be passed from generation to generation. All of our children will learn them. They'll be performing my dances and songs long after my spirit leaves this planet. But your canoes will float only until they're old. Then they'll rot."

Gat shrugged and went on with his work. He, too, was angry.

After a while, the brothers did not spend much time together. Each believed he was better than the other. When they did speak, they argued.

Chief Always-Laughs saw what was happening and worried.

"What is wrong with those two?" he asked his wife, Gitsemma. "They are always in a battle. They should get along."

Gitsemma shrugged. "Boys will be boys."

"It does not feel right, all the same," Chief Always-Laughs replied.

The boys' parents gave them time outs and took away their treats trying to make them behave but Gat and Ayuk kept fighting with each other. They played tricks on each other.

Once, when Gat was helping finish off a canoe, the leader of the canoe-makers told him to ask his brother to give a ceremonial dance at noon the next day. Gat told Ayuk to be at the canoe-building site at dawn.

Ayuk had to wait six hours before it was his turn to dance.

Another time, the canoe-makers told Ayuk to tell Gat that the group was starting to carve a new canoe the next morning. Instead, Ayuk told Gat that the canoe-makers asked him to find a good cedar during the next two days. Gat wandered off into the woods to look for a good canoe tree. By the time he came back, the canoe-makers had finished carving without him.

Ayuk and Gat tried to out-fish, out-hunt and out-trap each other.

Chief Always-Laughs warned them:

"It's no good spending your spirit trying to make your brother feel stupid. You must learn to work together. It seems to me that you are more interested in out-doing each other than you are in doing good for the tribe. Take care you do not find yourselves killing animals just to prove yourselves, rather than listening to see if their spirits are ready to join yours as food."

"Sure, sure," the boys said as they ran away. The last thing they wanted to hear was one of grandfather's lectures.

Ayuk and Gat continued to work against each other. Everything was a contest.

Whenever Gat finished a canoe, he would talk for days about how useful he had been and how much the canoe-makers needed him. Whenever Ayuk prepared for a new dance, he would talk for days about how his work would always be remembered.

They even turned meals into competitions. Ayuk tied to eat more than Gat. Gat tried to eat more than Ayuk. They both ate too much and gained weight. Then, they both went on a diet and became weak because they ate too little.

Gat's canoe-making and Ayuk's performing suffered because the boys were more interested in beating each other than they were in learning their work.

As a result, one fall evening after dinner their lives changed.

The tribe sat around the fire to hear songs and watch the dancers. Outside, the night air was crisp, with a hint of frost. The ground crackled with fresh-fallen leaves. Inside, it was warm and comfortable. The flames were high and the cook pots were full. As Grandmother Gitsemma began to explain a totem, Ayuk started to show off. He banged a drum and stamped his feet. He wanted everybody to see his new dance and hear his new song.

Gat sat with his back against a wall, banging rocks together as he made a new knife. He tried to be louder than his brother.

It was hard to hear Gitsemma's voice over the racket. It was even harder for people to talk to each other. Gat and Ayuk were making too much noise.

Ayuk stamped his way close to Gitsemma as she tried to finish her words.

She stopped telling her story and looked up at him.

"Please, Ayuk," she said. "I like your dance. But the children can't hear what I'm saying."

Gat saw another chance to make his brother feel like a fool.

He jumped to his feet.

"Yeah! You are making too much racket!" Gat shouted. "And you look like a goofy bird that's lost its nest. Nobody's impressed!"

Ayuk lost his temper. He ran around the fire and jumped on top of Gat. They rolled over and over trying to hit each other. Everyone around the fire had to jump to their feet to get out of the way. The youngest children started to cry.

The brothers were so busy fighting that they didn't realize they were rolling next to the fire. Ayuk had Gat underneath him and Gat tried to kick himself free. Gat's feet flashed out and caught the tripod that supported a cook pot. It spilled. Soup splashed all over the floor, made the fire spit and sizzle and sprayed three of the cooks with hot liquid. They jumped up shouting and one of them knocked a cedar table into the fire.

Suddenly the lodge was filled with smoke and sparks. The men ran out to the river to bring back buckets of water to dump on the burning cedar blankets, baskets and boxes.

Luckily, they were able to put out the flames before the lodge and everything in it burned to the ground. All the same, many beautiful carvings were ruined. Many cedar blankets, woven from root fibers to keep out the winter's cold, had to be thrown out.

Chief Always-Laughs was not laughing at all.

He was still covered with soot when he demanded that his grandsons stand before him. The rest of the tribe sat silently against the scorched walls of the lodge.

Chief Always-Laughs was red in his face. His voice was loud and hoarse from the smoke.

"Your fighting could have destroyed our home!" he cried. "Your spirits have become too small. You think only of yourselves and let your anger eat your knowledge. It is time you learned a good lesson!"

Gitsemma touched Chief Always-Laughs on his shoulder.

"Husband, husband," she pleaded. "Don't let your anger eat your wisdom. They are only boys."

The boys' mother and father said nothing. They knew Ayuk and Gat had to face the consequences of their behavior.

Chief Always-Laughs glared at Ayuk and Gat. His eyes were dark and he scowled.

"Take your knives and blankets — if you can find any that are not scorched — and leave this house," he told them. "You will take the canoe nearest the lodge and you will paddle north to the island of banishment in the shadow of the great mountain. Tonight, the moon is showing her full face and she will start to turn away. She will soon look like the curved bow of a canoe. Then she will begin to turn back. You will live on your own on the island until the next time her full face smiles upon the earth.

Gitsemma looked worried. Ayuk and Gat were stunned. Banishment was a punishment they had seen given men much older than they were. Under the banishment law, people who did something wrong were sent away until the spirits of the woods and waters taught them how to do the right thing.

"They're too young," Gitsemma murmured. "And the nights are cold."

"They've become old enough in their selfish ways," Chief Always-Laughs snapped back. "They'll learn how to live in the world and with each other."

He pointed to the door.

"Go!" he shouted at Ayuk and Gat.

Gat and Ayuk took their knives and blankets and left their grandfather's lodge. Nobody spoke to them as they prepared to leave but Gitsemma made sure their blankets were in good shape and their knives sharp.

Both boys had big knots in their throats, and they were trying hard not to cry. They tried not to look at each other.

Quietly they trudged away from their warm and cozy home down to the river bank.

Together, they pushed the canoe into the water. Together they began to paddle up the river. Night was falling. The island was a dark gray shape against the dark green water. The mountain looked like a jagged white tooth against the pale purple sky.

They knew they needed to get to the island as quickly as possible.

"I can paddle faster than you can!" Ayuk announced. And he paddled with all of his strength.

Gat, caught off guard, could not match Ayuk's speed, so the canoe went around in a circle and was hit broadside with a wave. It almost tipped over.

"Oh-oh," said Ayuk, and stopped paddling. "Grandfather was right. We must work together."

The rest of the way to the island was easy and quick because Ayuk and Gat paddled together in an even and strong rhythm.

It was almost dark by the time they reached the rocky beach of the island of banishment. They were scared and were getting cold.

They quickly built a fire. There was no time to argue. Gat picked up wood he knew to be dry. Ayuk twirled a piece of hard wood into a soft log to make sparks to start the fire.

Gat found two forked branches on a nearby cottonwood. Ayuk found a straight branch that could be used as a pole across the forks. Ayuk's blanket became a tent, stretched across the pole and weighted down with rocks.

They wrapped Gat's blanket around themselves to keep warm. They had no time to find food before only the light of the fire kept away the coldness and the blackness of the night.

They held each other tightly, and went to sleep. They were both hungry, and they knew they would need all of their strength to find food in the morning. The next full moon was a long time off and they knew frost would whiten the ground before they could go home. They needed to build a better shelter, find stores of food and get prepared for many cold and rainy days and nights.

Luckily, it did not rain the next morning. It was chilly, but the pale sun soon burned away the clouds resting on the water. Gat and Ayuk found ripe salmon berries and ate them for breakfast as they stirred the embers of their fire until it blazed.

"We need shelter," Gat said. "I can find the trees with the best bark."

"I can weave the bark into coverings for walls and a roof," Ayuk said.

"While you weave the bark, I will carve a fish hook," Gat promised.

"I'll dig for mussels," Ayuk replied.

So the boys learned how to work together because they needed each other to survive. Between them, they built a snug enclosure to keep out the rain. They ate fish they roasted over the fire and picked the end-of-season salmon berries and huckleberries. Gat carved a cedar pot that could hold water. Ayuk made hot nettle tea.

It rained almost every day but Ayuk and Gat dried out by the fire. The cedar bark roof of their structure protected them from the elements. When the winds from the sea grew stronger, they moved the shelter further away from the water and built it under trees and bushes.

Each day, they sat by their morning fire and decided what each should do until night fell so they could eat and stay warm. They worked together like a team and by the time the half-moon hung on the horizon, they knew they would be all right. They knew they could last until it was time to go home.

More days passed and each day the moon grew fatter in the night sky. Gat and Ayuk were proud of themselves. They had made themselves comfortable. They had food, shelter, and a crackling fire. After dark, they amused each other telling stories and they never argued. However, as more time passed, they began to feel homesick. They missed their families, and they ran out of stories to tell each other. One evening, they found themselves sitting in silence by the fire, feeling bored.

"We should play a game," Gat said.

Ayuk brightened up. "Yes. What should we do?"

Gat looked around for an idea. The river below the bank rippled with salmon. It was time for the fish to return to their breeding place and make new baby salmon. Their silver backs humped above the water.

"Let's place a marker on the beach and see how fast the salmon can swim," Gat suggested.

"How can we do this?" Ayuk asked.

"You stand downstream, pick one out and start counting. I will see how many counts it takes before it reaches the marker."

Ayuk laughed," O.K.," he said. "But it is getting dark. How can we tell which one we are timing?"

Gat thought a moment. "We must mark them somehow."

Ayuk said, after a minute. "Perhaps we could mark them with torches."

Gat looked at him. "Torches?."

"Yes," Ayuk replied. "We carve some sticks so that one end is pointed like an arrow and the other end is frayed. We light a small fire at the start point on the beach. Then we can light one of end of the arrow and spear a salmon with the other end. We could see how fast the salmon swims by the light it carries."

Gat smiled.

"That's a great idea," Gat said. "But if we spear a fish and it dies and we do not use its spirit to feed our body, we might offend it."

"Aw, come on," Ayuk said. "There's so many of them. Most of them will die before they reach their breeding place. If we kill a few, it will be easier for the ones that are left to survive.

"Okay," Gat said.

The boys built a fire on the beach and speared salmon with burning sticks. Some of the torches went out as the salmon dove, but others stayed burning as the dying fish floated to the surface and were pushed along by other fish flashing past the blaze.

The river, lit by orange flames, shone with the salmon oil on its surface. Dark shadows in the water made strange shapes. Gat thought he saw boats with white sails. Ayuk though he saw the shape of a headless bird, with smoke pouring from pods beneath it wings, skimming through a dark and moonless sky.

As it grew later, a cloud covered the moon and the boys were tired. They left the fire burning on the beach and curled up in their shelter. Their dreams were strong and frightening and they woke each other up because their dreams of fire and sadness made them cry out in their sleep.

The next morning the beach was littered with blackened twigs and the rotting bodies of salmon. The morning sun made the smell strong. Gat and Ayuk, feeling guilty, threw the sticks into the water and tried to bury the salmon so the stink would go away but they could not dispose of them all.

Black ravens came in a cloud and dove from the sky. With beaks as sharp as spearheads, they tore the salmon to pieces. Suddenly, the birds cawed as if they were screaming a warning and in mass of dark, beating feathers, wheeled down river away from the mountain. Gat and Ayuk shivered, it felt strange. Not only had the ravens gone but no bird was heard anywhere nor did the wind blow. There was no sound at all.

"Look at that!" Gat cried.

A cloud that looked like a white eagle feather rose in a giant plume from the mountain's peak.

"The mountain is smoking a peace pipe," Ayuk said. "It isn't angry."

Gat looked doubtful.

That evening, as the boys sat by the fire, again they were bored but they didn't want to race salmon that night. The smell was still with them.

"That was a dumb idea, of yours," Gat grumbled. "It stinks here."

"That was not my idea!" Ayuk cried. "We both thought of it!"

"Two people can't think one thought," retorted Gat.

"They can too!" shouted Ayuk.

A little frog hopped into the firelight. Its eyes glowed like jewels. Gat glared at Ayuk. His eyes, too, gleamed. Gat wanted to fight Ayuk and Ayuk was ready to fight him back.

A breeze billowed from the water and flames crackled higher. A spark flew from the fire and landed on Ayuk's leg.

Ayuk leaped to his feet. The burning sting on his leg was too much for him.

"You're a stupid, stupid person!" he shouted at Gat.

Gat grabbed the frog and threw it at Ayuk. It fell in the flame and exploded, pieces of the frog hit Ayuk.

Another frog came close to Ayuk. Its eyes seemed to be crying. Ayuk didn't care. He threw that one into the fire and its pieces hit Gat. Gat jumped up.

The earth rocked and swayed. There was a huge echoing rumble, louder and longer than any roll of thunder. A great wind scattered the fire and blew away the shelter. Ayuk and Gat screamed and ran toward the beach in the sudden darkness. Grit stung their skin. They tasted ashes in the air.

They could not speak above the roar. They could not hear and they could not see. The air burned their eyes and throats. The earth rocked and moved beneath their feet as they threw themselves into the canoe. Water steamed and rose around them. They could not breathe and they lost consciousness. The canoe stayed afloat despite the way it bucked and rocked in the raging river that rushed away from the flaming ground.

Ayuk and Gat remained unconscious. Their eyes were shut and their breathing faint. Behind them the trees blew flat and it rained ashes as the mountain blew its jagged, white top high into the night sky. Fire ran down the mountain's sides.

As they slept, Gat and Ayuk dreamed of a woman in a flaming gown weeping for her children. They saw a river of flames eat away the land and they saw their family's home burn and blow away.

Their canoe reached the sea and then was taken by the ocean's currents down the coast for many miles. Finally, it washed ashore on a beach where Gat and Ayuk were found by another tribe called the Chinooks. The boys awoke in a strange lodge, surrounded by strange people and far from their home and they could not remember who they were or where they came from.

When the mountain blew up, Chief Always-Laughs had been standing on the beach looking toward the peak and the island where Gat and Ayuk had been banished.

He saw the pillar of fire rising high into the sky.

"Oh no!" he cried. "I've lost my grandchildren!" He put his hands on his head and tears fell. Gitsemma ran to him. She held him and wept with him.

"We must all go!" she cried. "The water will run from the fire in a great wave!"

Chief Always-Laughs and all his people hurried to their canoes, paddled to the sea and headed north, away from the volcano. They landed on higher ground, built a new village and took the Raven as their new totem.

Chief Always-Laughs did not smile again for many years. Then, one day, a visiting man who had been fishing in the southern waters with the Chinook tribe, talked about two boys who had been found in a canoe after the volcano. He said they had no memory of who they were and where they came from. The man wondered if the Raven tribe knew who they might be.

Chief Always-Laughs and the boys' father went to visit the Chinooks and recognized Ayuk and Gat. They helped them remember their old home and what had happened to them. Ayuk and Gat were glad to find out who they were but because they had lived with the Chinooks for so many years, their home now was where they had landed. They stayed with the Chinooks, and Chief Always-Laughs returned to Gitsemma and the Ravens.

Artists in both tribes carved the weeping totems to remind their children that anger and wasting life, even that of the smallest frog can destroy the world we know.

Credit: Frog below and volcano woman with cane from Marius Barbeau: *Haida Myths Illustrated by Argillite Carvings.*

The Salmon Princess and the Bear Prince

Totem poles bearing the shapes of bears and salmon are part of the scenery from Alaska to Washington State. They show how people from two worlds became one family with a shared culture.

According to legend, the first group hiked to Alaska from Siberia. They crossed mountains and glaciers and along deep canyons and settled inland where they were helped by the spirits of the bear and the wolf. The second group paddled across the Pacific Ocean from Mongolia and settled on the coast near the Bering Sea where they were helped by the spirits of the salmon and the eagle.

In the beginning they did not trust each other at all. They fought every time they met.

The Salmon People warned their children to stay away from the Bear People.

"They'll capture you and eat you!" they said.

The Bear People growled a similar warning at their youngsters.

"The Salmon People will grab you and drown you!" they said.

Then, by accident, two young people changed history.

One of them was Riso, the only daughter of the Larkibu, the chief of the Salmon Tribe. The other was Zaradil, the oldest son of Kloos, the chief of the Bear Tribe.

Riso's parents told her how the tribe's ancestors had lived across the wide ocean and wore cone-shaped copper caps and how they brought copper headgear, ornaments and statues in their canoes to their new country as well as the knowledge of how to mine copper. Riso learned how to weave cedar fiber into cone-shaped hats very much like those worn by the ancestors.

Zaradil's parents told him how his ancestors battled tigers and followed wolves over mountain ranges of solid ice. He learned how to build sturdy shelters out of wood, stone or ice.

Larkibu, Riso's father, gave her everything she wanted. Riso was princess of the Salmon People and her father made sure her life was easy.

She had cedar boxes for her jewelry and she had her own canoe for pleasure trips.

While others in the tribe cooked the food and dried the salmon for winter food, Riso did not have to help. She liked performing the dances and the songs that welcomed the sacred first run of salmon but she did not like the slimy work of preparing the fish for drying.

Her father loved her singing and dancing.

"You're like the moon," Larkibu told his daughter. "You shine in the dark. Your singing brings light to our hearts."

When Riso wasn't singing, she was talking. She believed she was very wise and that everything she said was important. She had opinions about everything. Sometimes she hurt people's feelings because she made comments about their looks when she thought they were too fat or too thin. She criticized the way people did their hair or the way they wore their clothes.

She became known as Riso, the babbler.

The older women in the tribe shook their heads and worried.

"Riso is very beautiful," they said. "But she talks too much. She knows nothing."

Chief Larkibu just smiled at his daughter.

"Your voice is as beautiful as the ripples in a babbling brook," he told her.

"Babbling is what she does best," said the women.

There was nothing more they could do. The chief was rich and powerful and they could not offend him by insulting his daughter.

Riso's best friend was a girl called Mais. Mais was quiet by nature and too short and plump to be considered beautiful but she was kind. When Riso insulted her, Mais was not hurt. When Riso talked so much that people fell asleep with boredom, Mais felt sorry for her.

One year, as the summer ended and everybody was busy getting ready for the cold weather to come, Riso, who did not want to do any real work, offered to pick salmonberries for the tribe.

In this way she could avoid drying fish or weaving blankets.

"At least she's making some contribution," muttered the other women.

"Come with me, Mais," Riso cried. "I need your company!"

Mais looked doubtful; she had many chores to do.

After a second, Mais' mother nodded but warned: "Be sure you only pick berries close by on our lands. You don't want to be grabbed by the bears."

"Sure, sure," Riso cried as she ran outside. Mais followed her into the sunshine.

The bushes near the family lodge had been picked over already. The remaining berries were on hard-to-reach branches.

"These are no good!" Riso cried. "It'll take forever to fill our baskets."

She ran deeper into the forest. Mais ran after her.

"We shouldn't go so far!" Mais cried.

"We can if we want," Riso said. "The best berries are up in the high ridges."

She bounded along the narrow trail, happily breathing the fall air with its snap of frost to come.

The long grass beside the trail was a yellow cloud against red sumac leaves and purple vine-maples.

"Come on!" Riso cried. "The air is so fresh. It is much better to be out here instead of in that stuffy old lodge with all those stuffy old people."

Mais was worried.

"No. We're out here in the woods where we could be grabbed by the Bear People," she said.

"They wouldn't dare," Riso replied.

The two girls walked through a valley where devils' club and nettles grew thickly. They were forced to tread carefully so they would not get stung. They came to a grove of tree so tall the tops were almost invisible. The sun shone through the leaves with a strange, pale light.

After a while, they climbed a bluff and found a large patch of bushes loaded with the sweet salmonberries. Some were already dark red and nearly dry enough to be ground to paste.

Risu and Mais filled their baskets.

The air grew colder and the sun moved behind the trees.

"We'd best go home now," Mais said. "I don't want to be out here after dark. The Bear People are out at night."

"Why are you afraid of them?" Risu asked. "They are really stupid. They look weird too."

Mais looked around nervously.

"Hush," she said. "They could be in the woods listening."

"Yeah, right." Riso replied. "Anyway, so what if they are? Like I'm afraid of someone who's just one step above a wild animal?"

Mais sighed sadly.

"Oh, Riso," she said. "You'll never learn. Let's get out of here. Okay?"

The girls began to climb down the bluff. Going up had been easy but going down was tougher. They had to carry their loaded baskets over sand that slid on flat pieces of shale. Mais walked carefully, testing where she put her feet.

Riso scampered on ahead. She was about halfway down when her foot slipped and she fell. She rolled over and over to the bottom of the hill, bouncing off rocks and spilling berries in every direction.

Riso lay stunned on a patch of rough moss. Mais hurried to her side.

"Oh, oh!" Mais cried. "Are you all right?"

Riso sat up groggily.

"I don't know," she said. "My ankle hurts."

She pulled her foot toward her. It was already starting to swell up.

"Can you walk on it?" Mais asked. "You'll have to try."

Riso tried to stand up, but fell back with a cry.

"I can't. It hurts too much."

"Well, get up on the other foot. You can hop home. I'll support your other side," said Mais.

Riso shook her head.

"I can't," she said. "It hurts."

"You have to try," Mais said. "I can't leave you here."

"Just go get someone," Riso pleaded. Tears of pain ran down her cheeks. "Have Daddy bring me a litter."

"You could try walking. I can hold you up," Mais begged. "I've seen other people limp home on the shoulder of a friend. We're not that far."

"No," Riso said, lying back down on the moss. "I'm hurt. Now please stop being stupid. Go!"

Mais stood up and said reluctantly, "Okay. I'll hurry."

"You better," Riso grumbled.

Mais ran off through the woods. Riso lay back and shut her eyes trying not to think of the pain that throbbed through her ankle.

With her eyes still shut, she heard a strange sound. There was rustling and a crashing in the bushes to her right. Then she heard a growl.

Without opening her eyes, she wrapped her arms around her head.

"Go away!" she cried. "Shoo! Whatever you are!"

The growling grew louder, and the sound of twigs snapping under heavy feet grew closer.

She lay there trembling. Whatever it was came crashing out of the bushes. It stood above her and growled.

"Don't eat me! Please don't eat me!" begged the princess hiding her eyes.

Then Riso was surprised by the sound of laughter. She looked up. Standing above her, dressed in a bearskin cloak, was a young man. His leather shoes were edged with claws so that his footprints looked like those of a large grizzly.

Riso's eyes traveled from the claws on his feet to the thick, long black hair that fell to his shoulders.

She did not think he was good looking. His skin was dark, his cheekbones were high and his eyes were the color of charcoal. He had a long and pointed nose, not at all like the flat noses that Riso thought were handsome. He was very muscular and not very tall. Riso preferred young men who were tall and slender. She glared at him.

"Who are you?" she asked crossly. Now that she realized he was human, she stopped being afraid. She believed the Bear People would not dare to hurt a princess of the Salmon Tribe.

The young man scowled at her.

"I'm Zaradil, Prince of the Bears," he said, with a proud and unfriendly tone.

Although Riso didn't understand the words he was saying, she understood that he was introducing himself.

Riso sat up, trying to look as dignified as she could, knowing than her face was probably smudged with dirt. She pointed to herself.

"I am Riso, Princess of the Salmon People," she announced. "You may take me home to my father."

Zaradil snorted. Riso thought the sound very unpleasant and rude.

Riso gulped. She could tell that this Bear person was not impressed by her.

"My father will have his revenge if you hurt me or kidnap me," she told Zaradil.

Zaradil thought her tone indicated she was a high-born Salmon girl although he did not understand what she said.

He grabbed her arm and pulled her to her feet.

Riso's anger overcame her fear.

"I am princess of the Salmon People. We are much smarter than people who live like hairy, smelly animals!" she cried, although she knew he didn't speak Salmon.

Zaradil looked down at her. Riso's golden eyes flashed with fire and her thick red-brown hair tumbled to her waist. The circles under her angry eyes were purple against her pale skin. Her right foot was twisted and swollen. He felt sorry for her.

Riso felt she was in real danger. She had been injured in Bear country and she'd been told that Bear People have no pity for anybody. She looked into his eyes and thought maybe that this Bear prince was kinder than the others.

Zaradil picked her up in his arms. Riso gasped when she realized how strong he was. She felt as light as a feather as he carried her away. His passage over the rough ground made her ankle throb with pain. She tried to ignore it but a small cry escaped her lips as he climbed over a particularly large outcropping.

Zaradil stopped and looked down at her. Her chin was stubborn, but a tear had leaked from her eye. He walked more slowly through the dense underbrush, trying not to shake her too much.

Riso knew they were heading farther and farther away from the sea. The forest was dark and smelled damp. The salt smell of the ocean had faded. The berry bushes and grasses gave way to thick creepers and tall salal bushes. Fallen stumps were thickly covered with yellow-green moss. Pale gray moss hung from tree branches. The ground was red with bark and Zaradil made no sound as he moved along an almost invisible trail.

The sun sank low behind the trees. The forest grew dark. Riso shivered. An owl hooted in the distance; it sounded sad.

Zaradil felt her shiver and felt guilty.

Eventually, they came to a huge lodge built into the side of a cliff, surrounded by tall trees. A stream gurgling down the cliff had been diverted so that it ran by the entrance to the lodge. Smoke puffed from a hole in the roof.

Zaradil's father, Kloos, a fierce-looking man with a long, black beard and a bushy moustache, was outside the lodge leaning on a tall spear. He scowled as Zaradil approached.

"What's that?" Kloos growled.

"I've kidnapped a Salmon woman," Zaradil announced. His tone was brave, but Riso sensed he was nervous.

"Hmm," Kloos replied. "What are we supposed to do with her?"

"We can keep her until her tribe pays us in copper," Zaradil replied.

Riso gasped. She heard the word copper, which was the same in both languages. She wondered how the Bear People knew that her family had copper. She knew her father would never give it up without a fight.

Kloos grunted.

"Maybe. If she's worth anything," he said. "Bring her in."

Riso noticed that all the people in the lodge were wearing animal pelts, fur side out. They wore necklaces of bone and teeth. The men carried spears and long knifes hung from belts around their waists.

She shrunk against Zaradil as he carried her to the back of the lodge. This opened into a large cave with many sections and rocky ledges.

Some ledges covered by furs were clearly sleeping areas. Other ledges looked like storage for sharp rocks, spears and swords. Zaradil put her down in a sleeping area and walked away into the smoke. Riso gazed at the unfamiliar world inside the lodge. Bear hides were stretched on planks. Some women scraped the fat and the meat from the skins and threw the scrapings into a bubbling cook pot that swung over a smoky fire. Others pummeled and stretched the scraped skins to make them soft.

Riso lay back as tears welled from her eyes. Her ankle was a pure, throbbing lump of pain. She was frightened but was determined not to show it. She knew her father would give anything he owned to have her back but the copper did not belong to him. It belonged to the whole tribe and they would have to decide if she was worth it.

I wish I'd been a nicer person, Riso thought sadly. Not many people like me. They might think I'm not worth any copper.

Then, the smallest and thinnest woman Riso had ever seen tiptoed through the smoke toward her.

The woman wore a soft gray fur hat and a floor-length gray fur gown. Her hat was held in place by a pair of large round ears that sprung out on either side of a little, wrinkled, but friendly face. The woman's eyes were surprisingly large and jet black. Her nose was small, round and very pink.

"Who are you?" Riso asked.

The women sniffed and her nose twitched. She understood the question.

"I'm Seets," she said in a thin and squeaky voice. Seets reached out and grasped Riso's throbbing foot with hands like dark-brown claws. But they were gentle as they encircled the ankle that was three times its normal size and bulged purple above Riso's leather slipper.

As Seets tried to move Riso's foot, Riso cried out in pain.

"That's broken, my girl," Seets squeaked in a whisper. "We'll have to splint it."

Riso's could not understand what the mouse-like woman said but she sense that she was kind and wanted to help her.

At least there are nice people here, Riso thought. I'm no good to anybody. How could I have been so stupid?

Seets scurried away. Riso curled into a ball. A tear ran down her cheek. In a few moments, Seets came back with a bowl of ground bark soaked in water, leather strips and smooth pieces of wood.

She handed the bowl to Riso.

Riso recognized the bark as the type also used by her family's medicine man when people were hurt. She drank the liquid and it began to work right away, diminishing her pain. I can be tough, she told herself. I'll not show how much it hurts. I'll be safer around these strangers if they think I am strong.

Seets pulled on the swollen ankle until it snapped into place. A flash of fiery pain shot up Riso's leg. She bit her lower lip and did not cry out.

After that, the pain was manageable. Seets tied the leather strips around the wooden splints on either side of Riso's broken ankle.

"Now it will get better," Seets told her. "You must rest it for a few weeks."

Riso, exhausted, lay back and fell asleep. She slept until morning when she was woken up by Seets bringing her a bowl of wild turnip soup.

The Search Begins

By the time Mais had returned to the Salmon lodge to get help for Riso, it was dusk. Although Larkibu and Riso's older brother, Niska, grabbed a litter and followed Mais into the fading light, it quickly became too dark to see the trail. Mais, in tears, could not lead the men to the spot where Riso had fallen.

"She probably found shelter under a bush. The nights aren't that cold yet," Larkibu said, but his heart was heavy.

Just before dawn the next morning, Larkibu and Niska and Grandmother Hally, set out once again to find Riso. Grandmother Hally had magical powers and could foretell the future and might be able to see what happened to Riso.

Mais led the group to the salmonberry bush where she had left Riso. They found her basket with the salmonberries spilled onto the ground. They noticed the place Riso had fallen and picked up shreds of her dress from the rocks. Alongside her tracks, on either side, they saw the claw marks that were Zaradil's footprints.

"Oh no!" Larkibu cried. "The grizzlies got my Riso!"

"She's dead by now, I bet," Niska said sadly.

Grandmother Hally bent down and rubbed the ground where Riso had fallen. Then she rubbed the claw mark.

"She's not dead," Hally said. "She'll be back with us, I know this. We must keep looking for her."

The Salmon People began to follow faint tracks into the deep woods as rain began to fall.

Little Bears on the Trail

Meanwhile, Zaradil's youngest brothers, Gunet and Myet, were rounded-eyed with awe when Zaradil told the family how he had captured the salmon girl. They worshipped their older brother and spent their lives trying to do what he did.

"Let's help him," Gunet said.

"How?" Myet asked.

"Well, we can go back to where he found her."

"We must be sure to erase our tracks and his," Myet said, remembering what they had been taught.

"For sure," Gunet said. "Then we follow the salmon girl's tracks back to her home and return here with directions to the lodge of the Salmon People. Then Dad will know where to send our warriors for the copper."

"We're small so it'll be easier for us to stay hidden," Myet said.

"We'll just get the directions and come back. We won't get captured. We'll be as silent as wolves," Gunet agreed.

The boys put on their Bear-cub cloaks and set off as the sun hid behind thick, gray clouds. Rain misted the leaves of the tall trees as the Salmon People searchers and the Bear-cub boys headed toward each other on the same trail.

About five miles from the Bear People's cave, a massive cedar tree had fallen across the trail and split into two pieces. On one side of the trail, bright green hemlock seedlings and golden mushrooms sprouted from the gray wood of the stump. On the other side of the trail, yellow moss and red vines covered the fallen top half of the tree.

Gunet and Myet suddenly found themselves face-to-face with Larkibu and his group as they entered the trail between the sections of the broken cedar tree. The boys gulped and looked at each other. Larkibu and Niska looked down at them. They looked like little brown bear cubs.

"Who are you?" Larkibu asked. "What are you?"

What are these people saying? Gunet wondered. "We are the people of the Bear," he growled back as deeply as he could.

These Bear cubs don't even speak a language anyone can understand, Larkibu thought.

Gunet and Myet exchanged glances. They didn't want the Salmon People to realize how close they were to the Bear cave. Perhaps they could drive them away.

Gunet growled and tried to hit Larkibu. Myet did the same to Niska.

Larkibu grabbed Gunet and Niska grabbed Myet.

They held the wriggling and yelling boys as rain began to fall heavily.

"What will you do with these?" Mais asked.

Hally looked up at the dark and swollen sky. Wind roared in the swaying tree tops.

"If we let them go, they might lead us to their people," Niska yelled.

Hally shook her head.

"Not these two," she shouted over the wind. "They'll lead us in circles until we get lost. And a big storm is coming. The wind is singing to me that Riso is safe and will be kept safe. "

"Then we'll take them back with us. Their families will look for them and perhaps we can trade them for Riso," Larkibu said. "Or, when the weather clears, perhaps they will lead us to her." He squinted up at the blackening sky. "But we have to get back now before we can't see our way out of here. Are you sure Riso is safe?"

"As sure as this storm rages," Hally shouted back.

Larkibu and Niska covered the boys' heads with their fur cloaks and tied the sleeves behind them so they would easier to carry.

Fat rain drops drenched the ground. The trail ran with mud, leaves and rocks. By the time the group reached the hillside where Riso had fallen, a small river was rushing over the sandy shale. The water uprooted berry bushes and erased the trails and any sign of human passage.

The boys, their heads covered and protected from the pelting rain by their cloaks didn't notice that their tracks were being washed away. They didn't see the signal Larkibu gave his men who met them on the way to the Salmon lodge. The boys were surprised and had no time to fight back when Larkibu's men grabbed them and dragged them away to a small hut near the lodge.

"What's happening?" Gunet asked, frightened. Myet tried not to cry.

They were pushed through the doorway and the door slammed shut behind them. They heard the bolt slide across the outside, locking them in. They wriggled out of their cloaks.

"We can't ever let them know where the Bear cave is," Myet whispered. "We must wait until Dad finds us. Then they can trade that Salmon girl for us."

As the days grew shorter, Larkibu led dozens of search parties through the forest, trying to find the fallen cedar tree where he had met the boys, hoping to track the Bear lodge from that point. But even the trail to the tree had been wiped out by mudslides and newly formed streams.

As fall storms turned to winter storms, Larkibu realized the snows would make finding Riso's trail impossible. Perhaps if he could understand the young Bear boys, they could tell him where his daughter might be.

He asked Mais to sit with them and teach them the language of the Salmon People. The boys learned quickly. In a month, Larkibu was able to question them.

Larkibu then realized the boys had no idea how to lead anybody back to their home. He still asked them for landmarks near the bear lodge that might help pinpoint its location. But Gunet and Myet refused to say anything about the land around their home. Larkibu was not a cruel man and he admired the boys for keeping their secrets.

Once, during questioning, Myet did lose his self control. Myet shouted that his family would come, rescue him and his brother, kill all the Salmon People and steal all their copper.

Larkibu was surprised to learn that the Bear People wanted copper. He decided to use Myet and Gunet as servants until he decided what to do with them.

"Those Bear People don't know where we live," Larkibu told the tribe. "If we can't find them, they can't find us. Meanwhile, we have time to prepare to defend ourselves and our copper. If they attack, we will be ready for them."

Weeks passed as Myet and Gunet kept busy cleaning the lodge and stacking the grass baskets of dried salmon. The boys were well treated by their captors but they were closely watched and were not given a chance to escape.

"It's not as bad as it could be," Gunet told Myet over a meal of clams, roots and berries. "They have some neat stories and we're learning lots of new things. And I'm sure we'll be rescued after the weather warms up."

Myet sighed. He was more homesick than his brother. "I hope so," he said.

Snow whitened the ground and heaped against the lodge. The Salmon People huddled around the fires and told their stories. Myet and Gunet heard about the giant raven who built the islands in the sea out of pebbles he dropped into the sea so he could rest and they learned about the giant clam from which all people came.

Larkibu sighed and stared into the fire, remembering how beautifully Riso had been able to sing. He wondered why Hally was so certain he would see his daughter again and hoped she was right.

Winter with the Bears

Until winter hit, Zaradil and the Bear People kept searching for Myet and Gunet but could not find their trail through the soaked and flooded mountains.

So, while the Bear brothers learned the work and language of the Salmon People, the captured Salmon princess, Riso, learned how to work with the Bear People and, taught by Seets, how to speak their language.

Seets was as patient as she was firm. She taught Riso how to pull the bear skins into material soft enough to be made into clothing and how to sew intricate patterns into the leather. At the same time, Riso showed Seets how to weave cedar into blankets and baskets.

During the short days of winter, Riso was still singing, but very softly, so she would not wake her captors. Chief Kloos and the rest of the Bear People huddled deep inside their cave house. Outside, snow fell and ice froze in jagged teeth that lined branches and the lips of rocks. When the winter work was done, the Bear People slept most of the day and all night. Riso became bored. Even Seets could not find enough for her to do.

One day, Riso sat alone in the entrance to the bear cave. Below her, snow lay like a glittering blanket crumpled around bushes and tree stumps. The sky was blue, the image of a white cloud floated in the blue water of a pond. A raven rose from a leafless tree and pushed his black wings into the frosty air.

Riso began to sing the song of the raven. The song told the story of how the raven found a glowing ball of light and threw it into the sky. The glowing ball became the moon and still lights the world at night.

Zaradil, who had been dozing inside by the fire, heard her voice and came to sit beside her.

He looked at her face. She is so beautiful, he thought. Her voice is sweet. When the song was over, he reached across and held her hand.

"You sing well," he said. "You are like the moon and light the world."

Zaradil's kind words reminded Riso of her father. Tears glistened on her cheeks and rolled onto the collar of the white fur coat she wore.

"What's the matter?" Zaradil asked.

"I wish I could go home," she said sadly. "Why can't I go home?"

Zaradil sighed. "Right now, if I could, I'd take you," he said. "My greed for your family's copper seems to have lost me my little brothers. I've angered the spirits. They sent rain, storms and now snow and ice to hide the trail."

Riso looked at him.

"My family can't find me here either?" she asked.

Zaradil shook his head. "I doubt it," he said.

Riso looked over the snow and ice and felt the warmth of the young man's hand around hers. Suddenly she knew what would happen. It was as if her grandmother's gift of telling the future had come to her.

She looked across at Zaradil.

"I'm not sure my family would have paid the copper anyway," she said.

"Why not? You're the chief's daughter."

Riso sighed. "The copper belongs to the whole family. It came from our ancestors across the sea. It has always been with us. I know they wouldn't want to give it up, especially for me."

"Why not?" Zaradil looked at her. She was so lovely. He knew he would have given his life for her.

"Nobody liked me much," Riso said slowly. "I talked too much, and I was lazy. I thought of myself first and didn't notice how anyone around me felt."

"That can't be true!" Zaradil said.

He had seen how much work Riso did, despite her bad foot. He had heard Riso teaching the younger children how to sing some of her songs and she was kind to little old Seets. Seets, who had often been lonely before Riso arrived, now was much happier and had nothing but good things to say about the beautiful young Salmon princess.

"It is," Riso said. "But I know better now. I wish I could go home and make things right."

Zaradil was silent for a few moments. The snow glittered like diamonds in the sunlight.

"I've learned something too," he said.

She looked at him curiously.

"You are worth more than any amount of copper. I had no right to kidnap you," he said slowly.

Riso felt safe beside him. She knew that he would help her.

"When the snows are gone, take me home," she said. "You can do it. You can remember where you found me. I can remember the way from there."

Zaradil smiled.

"As soon as the sun is warmer and the days are longer, I'll try," he said gently. "But let me talk to my father about it."

Zaradil's father, Kloos, leader of the bears, had been very unhappy since Myet and Gunet disappeared. He had never really wanted the copper and often felt that it had been wrong to kidnap Riso. He had grown to like Riso and worried that she was unhappy.

So when Zaradil and Riso asked him if Riso could go home in spring, he thought it was an excellent idea.

"Yes," the old man grunted. "It would be good if you took her back as soon as the snow melts. But you might not be able to find the way."

"We can," Zaradil said. "I can find the way to the place I found her. I'll use the skill of the wolf and the strength of the bear."

Riso said. "And I can find my way home from there. I'll use the eyes of the eagle and the instinct of the salmon. The salmon always knows the way home."

Kloos nodded. "So it shall be. Maybe if I send you home to your people, your salmon spirit will flow into my small sons Myet and Gunet, and they, too, will find their way home."

As soon as the snow was almost gone, the streams ran free and ferns curled like little fiddleheads above the ground, Zaradil and Riso packed supplies on their backs and headed down the mountain.

Zaradil walked carefully, sniffing the air and looking closely at the hills around him. The spirit of the wolf was with him, and he found the cliff where he had found Riso.

A waterfall roared over it. The trail, the path and the way down was gone. The fall rains, winter storms and the melting snow merged in a wide ribbon of white foam.

"How can we get down?" Riso wondered.

Zaradil said. "Get on my back."

He bent down and she climbed on. She held on to his shoulders and wrapped her legs around his waist. Zaradil had become even stronger during the winter rest. He was able to scramble down the side of the waterfall, slipping between the trees as sure footed as bear going down a canyon.

At the bottom, she climbed off his back and gave him a grateful hug. Zaradil sniffed the air.

"Now I can't tell you which way to go," he said.

Riso turned around slowly and looked down at the stream.

"I do," she said. "Mais and I got here from that direction," She set off, following the rocks along a stream that gurgled and sang down the slope. Zaradil followed easily.

The stream led the pair straight toward the sea. It was almost dark by the time Riso sniffed the air and laughed.

"It's the salt," she cried. "I can smell the salt. We are almost home!"

Families United

Larkibu was lighting his pipe by the evening fire when he heard something very familiar. He looked up and tears filled his eyes.

"The spirit of Riso is singing to me!" he cried. "My dear daughter has sent her spirit."

Myet and Gunet, who were eating sticky berry cakes, stopped chewing for a moment.

"It's not my spirit," Riso said as she crossed into the lodge from the doorway. "It's me, Dad."

Larkibu jumped to his feet and ran to his daughter. Myet and Gunet saw who was with her and ran to their brother. For a few moments everyone was hugging and shouting and laughing with happiness.

Once Zaradil and Riso had rested, they insisted on going with Larkibu to take the Bear brothers, Myet and Gunet back to their father, Kloos.

Larkibu and Kloos became good friends. Zaradil and Riso spent a lot of time together, and, in a couple of years, they married. They had twin sons.

The Bear People and the Salmon People became one family. Together they understood the spirit of the bear, the salmon, the wolf, and the eagle. When the moon was full, they sang the story of the raven and how the world began.

Once Zaradil and Riso had rested, they insisted on going with Larkibu to take the Bear brothers, Myet and Gunet, back to their father, Kloos.

Larkibu and Kloos became good friends. Zaradil and Riso spent a lot of time together, and, in a couple of years, they married. They had twin sons.

The Bear People and the Salmon People became one family. Together they understood the spirit of the bear, the salmon, the wolf and the eagle. When the moon was full, they sang the story of the raven and how the world began.

True Love's Journey to the World under the Sea

Totem poles showing a man, a woman, a whale, and an eagle told a classic love story.

Tana and Martin lived in a small cedar hut on an agate beach. Each day the tide came in over the colorful rocks and each day, when the tide went back out, the rocks gleamed like hundreds of jewels.

Tana's family knew the spirit of the whale. Martin's family knew the spirit of the owl. After Tana and Martin were married, they carved a whale and an owl into the totem pole before their home.

"We have the freedom of the whale, and the wisdom of the owl," they told each other.

Tana's childhood had not been easy. She had been born looking so different that at first sight of her baby Tana's mother cried. Her father was so upset that he threw his axe at a stump. Tana's hair was pale blond, almost white. Her eyes were gray as a stormy sea and her skin was as white as a washed barnacle.

"She's ugly!" Her mother wept. "She'll never find a husband!"

Tana's aunt, Nan, who was a wise woman, shook her head. "She is different, for sure," Nan said. "But this child has a special magic. She has the colors of the white whale who swims between the sea ice islands."

Martin was taller than all of his brothers and his black hair began to turn gray when his was still a boy. His family knew that before very long, like the high mountains, he would wear a crown of snow.

Martin and Tana met when he came to trade with her family. Tana was on the beach collecting shells. In the morning light, her hair was as silver as moonbeams on dark water. She saw Martin against the sun. His hair was as white as the surf and his shape was as dark and strong as a giant cedar against the sky.

They knew at once they were meant for each other and married only a few months later.

They decided they would not live with her family, as was the custom, but would build their own house on the beach.

At first, Tana and Martin were as happy as sandpipers chasing insects at low tide. They laughed like ravens in spring and believed their days would always be as golden as the first rays of dawn, as fresh as new pine needles and as free as the white puffed clouds in the summer-blue sky.

Their world changed one morning as Tana and Martin walked along the stony shore. Mountain peaks across the bay turned from purple to pink as they set careful feet around sharp shells and craggy drift logs. They held hands as they watched the sharp fins of whales rise between the spikes of white sea foam. Closer to the shore, a lazy otter turned on his back and sunned his stomach. He bobbed up and down on the waves as if he were made of dry wood. Seagulls wheeled through the clear air, dove to the beach to pick up mussels, smashed them on the rocks and gulped down their catch.

Tana smiled up at Martin. He smiled down at her. Tana inhaled the salty wind from the waves, let go of Martin's hand and ran ahead, laughing. She ran on and on. Her hair fluttered behind her like the white feathers of eagle wings. Her long legs were a blur.

Martin tried to catch up with her. Ahead of him, Tana looked half-bird, half-human. She rounded the corner of a cliff and disappeared. Then he heard her gasp and it seemed that a cloud covered the golden sun.

He followed her and founded her crouched, crying over a white and bloody shape on the beach.

"What is it?" he cried.

"Oh, look," Tana sobbed. "The poor creature!"

At her feet a snow-white sea otter trembled in pain. Its sad brown eyes gazed them as its spirit struggled.

"It's dying," Martin said.

"It's suffering," Tana added. "Look how badly it's been hurt."

A bloody tear above the otter's heart poured bright blood over the silver fur. It trembled and moaned.

"You've got to stop it from hurting," Tana said.

Martin took his dagger and plunged it deep into the otter's heart. The otter's eyes clouded and it lay still.

Tana's tears hung like diamonds on the otter's fur.

Martin looked down.

"This is a beautiful pelt," he said. "The otter hasn't died for nothing. It'll keep you warm this winter."

Tana nodded sadly. She turned away as Martin skinned the otter and stretched the fur out on nearby rocks.

Tana sighed and turned back to look at the fur.

"Oh, look!" she cried. "It's all bloody. It'll be stained."

"We couldn't help that," Martin said. "There was blood on the pelt from its injury."

"If I wash it right now in the sea, the stains won't be permanent," Tana told him.

She picked up the pelt and ran into the sea.

"Watch out!" Martin cried. "There's an undertow here. It'll pull you down!"

As he watched in horror, a huge wave rose like a glittering hill and crashed at Tana's knees. She bent to scrub the fur but lost her footing and disappeared. Martin ran to save her but couldn't reach her in time. He saw one white arm rise above the water. He saw her long hair blowing in the foam and then she was gone.

"Tana! Tana!" Martin's cries echoed over the dark waters. He saw the fins of a pod of killer whales.

"Please, Whale People! Find my Tana. Bring her back to me!"

The sun gleamed from one of the fins and turned it the color of copper.

Martin ran to his canoe and pushed it into the surf. There was no sign of her although he paddled out to sea and around the bay, knowing she was a strong swimmer and should have been able to reach the surface. She was gone, as were the whales.

Clouds rose from behind the hills and covered the sun. With steps as heavy as his heart Martin he walked to Tana's family's lodge to tell them what had happened.

Tana's family bent their heads and began to sing the spirit song. Tana's mother wept silently and her father buried his head in his hands. They did not blame Martin because the sea takes many people when it is their time.

Nan, Tana's aunt frowned, walked outside and went through the trees to a cedar that had been hollowed out by lightening. Its bark was covered with moss and there was a doorway to the room inside where the walls were lined with glistening black charcoal. Stars glittered through the opening in its top. Nan knelt and burned wild sage. She closed her eyes and asked the spirits of the cedar to tell her where Tana might be.

By the time Nan returned to the lodge, the family, exhausted by grieving, had gone to their sleeping areas. Only Martin remained awake. He sat alone, trying to see Tana's shape in the dying embers of the fire.

Nan sat beside him. Her heart ached for him. She took his strong brown hand in her little white one and whispered, "Tana has not left you."

Martin turned his sad eyes on her. "I know her spirit still lives," he said sadly. "But I need her touch, her laugh, her everything—" He buried his head in his hands and groaned.

Nan went on. "You saw a copper fin where she went into the sea. I had a dream as I slept in the sacred cedar. In that dream the earth spirit told me that Tana is alive both in body and spirit."

Martin stared at her. "She was swallowed by the sea! She's drowned!"

Nan shook her head. "That copper fin belonged to the Whale People," she said. "Their king swims with the power of that fin. He has taken her to his cave under the sea. He wants her to be his queen."

"His queen!" Martin cried. "She is my wife! How can I get her back? Where is this cave?"

"It's deep in the ice where the sea enters the land far north of here. If you cross the mountains and follow the northern star up the coast, you'll find the mouth of a wide river marked by a giant strand of kelp. You'll need to follow the kelp down through the water until you read the land of the whale."

"I'll freeze in that water!"

Nan handed him a little cedar box. "This box is full of fat given to us by a mountain goat who gave up his spirit for us. Before you dive, cover yourself with it. You'll stay warm. Leave after dawn but don't go alone."

"Who'll go with me?"

"Ask your cousins, Marmot and Swallow, to go with you to the kelp strand. Marmot is an excellent tracker and Swallow can make a canoe go so fast that it seems to fly over the water."

Martin jumped to his feet. "We can leave now!"

"Not yet. It's too dark." Nan said. "You need sunlight to cross those ridges. Talk to your cousins now but wait until dawn to leave."

Nan stood up, left the fire and went to her sleeping place.

There was no sleep for Martin. He woke up Martin and Swallow and asked them to help him find Tana. They agreed and went back to sleep. Martin spent the rest of the night packing and pacing. His carrier included the cedar box, his arrows, his spear and daggers, food and medicine stones.

He was outside waiting for his cousins as soon as night began to fade. Martin's heart was heavy but he told himself over and over again that Tana was alive and he would rescue her.

Behind the lodge, purple mountain ridges spiked pink layers of clouds against a mauve sky. Rose-colored mist ribbons snaked down canyons to the valleys.

After Martin watched the day brighten for half an hour, he decided he couldn't wait any longer. He began to walk along the trail. He had not gone far when he heard the sound of feet behind him.

Marmot and Swallow

"Wait up!" his cousins called. "We had to get the boat!"

Marmot and Swallow, carrying a canoe on their backs, caught up with him.

Marmot wore a cedar cloak dyed purple and Swallow's cloak was made of gray feathers. Martin smiled at them.

"Thanks for coming with me," he said. Marmot and Swallow grinned.

"We'll help you get Tana back," Marmot said cheerily. "You'll see."

So Martin, Marmot and Swallow began their long hike toward the pass that would lead to the other side.

The trail became steeper as they climbed between cedar and fir until they were almost at the snowline. Trees were smaller and twisted into strange shapes. Dark green vines clung to sand and rock. Tiny yellow mountain sunflowers, small white daisies, red Indian paintbrush and blue asters painted the high valley with bursts of color.

Martin was not moved by the beauty around him. He thought only of Tana. The three men walked in silence. They came to a river made from a melting glacier. It foamed over rocks, created pools and plunged hundreds of feet to the forest below. Martin cut down a young hemlock long enough to span the water.

Marmot jumped across the rocks dragging the tip of the tree across the water. It made a bridge so the three could carry the canoe to the other side.

They went on and up. They found the snow near the mountain's peak was frozen hard and lay flat and gleaming on the high valley ahead of them.

By dusk they were able to see their way down the other side. It was twisted and dangerous but it led to a great bay, hundreds of feet below them that had been cut into the mountains by the salt sea.

"Let's rest here," Swallow suggested. "We won't be able to find our way down in the dark."

They dug shelters in the snow and built a fire. The sun disappeared behind the mountain and the way down vanished into darkness.

Swallow and Marmot slept, but Martin stayed awake under the stars, aching for Tana.

At the first gleam of sunlight, the three were back on the trail down the mountain and by dusk they reached the shore of a bay. The sea lapped at the base of the ice cliffs that surrounded it. Every so often, a lump of ice as big as a house broke off and sank into the gray waters, with only its tip above the waves. Across the bay, they saw a small beach.

Swallow, Martin and Marmot pushed the canoe into the water. The waves looked like purple mountains capped with snow. Once they had paddled past the onshore breakers, the sea was as smooth as glass. The moon was full and the canoe looked as if it had been dipped in silver.

Softly, the paddles slipped into the smooth water and out again. For a long time, the only sound was the slap of the prow against the sea.

Then Swallow cried out: "Look there! Look there!"

The Sea Serpent

The giant coils of a sea serpent looped over the waves ahead of them.

"It's the dragon of the sea!" Marmot gasped. He knew the giant serpents lived in the deepest waters and had lived there long before humans grew on the planet. Martin stood up in the canoe, holding his dagger. Its small blade looked like a pin against the great green side of the monster.

"That dagger will do no good!" cried Swallow. "The dragon won't even feel it." The serpent's coils slithered closer. The three men felt as small as ants. Then, the serpent raised its head, water poured from the massive ridged forehead. The canoe rocked and the three men grabbed its sides so they would not be tipped into the water.

The serpent's great red eyes gazed at the terrified trio. For a few moments, nothing seemed to move.

Martin looked up at the serpent's eyes, now turning green in the moonlight. They held gentleness.

"Please," he begged. "The Whale People have captured my wife. I am going to find her. Please let us pass safely."

The great head of the serpent tilted to one side. It seemed to be listening. Martin thought fast. He remembered what he had been told about the giant serpent.

"I know you are the last of your kind and that you mate for life. I, too, have one love for my life. But my love has been taken away," he pleaded.

The serpent seemed to understand. It closed its eyes and dove to the bottom of the sea. The canoe rocked and lurched in the huge whirlpool left in its wake. For a few frightening seconds, the men fought to keep the canoe afloat in the tossing and twirling water. They paddled as hard as they could. Then, suddenly, the water was as smooth as glass, and the canoe floated quietly on the flat surface.

"Did we really see that thing?" Marmot asked.

Martin rubbed his finger along the side of the canoe. It was smeared with green slime.

"We saw it all right," he said. "But somehow, I don't think it wanted to hurt us."

"We're lucky," Marmot said. "We'd better get to shore and rest for the night. I'm wiped."

Suddenly, a thick fog surrounded them, as if a cloud had landed in the water and encircled them.

"Where's the shore?" Martin asked. Marmot sniffed. He pointed.

"That way," he said. "I can smell the damp earth."

The three cousins paddled in the direction he indicated and landed on a patch of soft sand under a cliff. There they built a small drift log fire and made a shelter from the canoe. Marmot and Swallow soon fell asleep.

Martin couldn't shut his eyes. He looked up at the stars and wondered if Tana was still okay.

By next morning, the fog was thicker. It was impossible to see more than a few feet.

"How'll we find our way in this?" Martin asked.

"I can scent my direction even in this weather," Marmot said. "But we will have to paddle close to the shore until it lifts."

The three pushed their canoe off the beach into the fog. Whiter than snow, it was like breathing frozen air. Frost coated their cloaks, their hoods, their hair and hands. The three cousins looked like ghosts slipping through the thick air. Each time they breathed out, a small puff of smoke came from their mouths and hung in the mist. Even the sounds of the paddles and the prow against the water were muffled by the fog. The silence was deep, eerie and thick.

After several hours it seemed that the fog was a little lighter and that shadows were forming in the direction of the shore. Martin pointed to the shapes. It was too cold to speak. Marmot and Swallow nodded. They turned the canoe toward the shapes on the shore, shimmering in the deep mist.

The fog was not as thick close to the beach and they saw that the shapes were caves rising above the rocky shale beach with black boulders capped by crowns of ice and snow. They saw no trees or bushes and no signs of life. It looked as alien as if it were another planet. Only the way the waves smashed against the shale and rose into plumes of foam looked familiar.

They kept paddling along the shoreline looking for a place to land. They listened, and above the smashing of the waves, they heard a strange pounding sound.

"What's that?" Marmot asked.

"Who knows," Martin said uneasily, searching for somewhere to beach the canoe. Along most of the shoreline the rocks and crags plunged straight into the sea. Only a few places were flat and smooth enough for a boat. The place they finally chose was marked by a single dead cedar that had managed to root itself but had finally been killed by the bitter salt wind. Now it stood, gnarled and knotted by the elements, like the skeleton of something that once lived, clawing at the sky with the few bare branches that had not already fallen at its feet.

"Firewood," Marmot observed. The eerie pounding sounds grew louder as they reached the beach and seemed to come from beneath the ice-coated rocks under their feet.

With stiff fingers, they pulled the canoe up on the bank. Martin pulled fire makings from his pack, twirled the fire stick into dry twigs, and soon they were able to warm their hands over a small fire. Swallow made a hot bark soup over the fire, and they soon were warm and strong again. The steady thumping from under their feet continued as they ate.

"What are those noises?" Martin wondered.

"They could be the echoes of waves against the cliffs or the sounds of underground rivers dumping into the ocean." Swallow said.

Martin looked at the craggy beach.

"Nan said one of those underground rivers leads to the hidden home of the whales. We should paddle along this shore until we find the underground river and its kelp marker," he said. "She said that's the only entrance to the Whale People's home. You drop me off at the marker and come back here. I'll find Tana, rescue her and bring her back to this old tree."

Marmot gasped, "You shouldn't go alone!"

Martin looked at him steadily.

"I must do this alone. Anyhow, one person would have the best chance to creep into the whale kingdom undetected."

Marmot looked out into the fog. It was retreating from shore and going further out to sea. He sniffed the damp air.

"The wind is blowing the fog away from the beach," Marmot said. "I think that kelp marker is much closer than we realize; it smells like whale around here."

Martin swallowed his hot soup. "Well, then, let's go. You take me to the kelp. Then come back and wait for me."

Swallow worried, "You'll freeze in that water."

"Martin said, "Nan gave me this box of mountain goat fat. I'll coat myself with it so I won't feel the cold."

"I sure hope that works," Swallow grumbled. "Do you have a weapon?"

"I have a dagger of black stone. It's very sharp," Martin said.

Marmot looked doubtful but saw that Martin was determined.

"Okay," Marmot said. "Let's go."

The three men packed their gear, climbed back into the canoe and paddled north. Martin hung over the prow, looking for the kelp. Suddenly he cried: "Stop! Look!"

The canoe was opposite the mouth of a wide black river. A fat strand of silver kelp floated up from the bottom. Its wide leaves scraped the bottom of the canoe.

Martin took out the little box of mountain goat fat and smeared himself from head to foot. When he was done, he glistened from head to foot and looked like a giant sea otter.

"I'm ready," he said. "You wait for me by that old tree. If I am not there in five days, paddle back home and tell the family that my spirit has left the planet. Please understand, I will not come back without Tana."

Marmot and Swallow nodded sadly as, without a ripple, Martin slipped like an eel into the icy water.

The Kingdom of the Whales

Martin pulled himself hand over hand down the kelp strand. He held his breath until it felt as if his lungs would burst. The kelp seemed to be endless and the water around Martin grew darker and darker. Then, just as he thought he would explode, he saw something glimmer ahead of him. The kelp snaked toward it. As fast as he could, using his last drop of energy, he pulled himself toward the light. Then, just as its source widened above the water, his foot hit sand. He stood up. His head burst into air and he took a shuddering breath.

He was in an underground cavern surrounded by sandy beaches. Glittering rocks hung from the roof overhead and piles of colored stones marked entrances to tunnels. Martin pulled himself into a niche and hid while he caught his breath.

He knew one of the entrances must lead to the whale cave and Tana. But which one?

He listened hard. Perhaps he could hear something. After a while, his patience paid off. He heard voices coming from a nearby tunnel. The voices were child-like, sad and became clearer as they grew closer. Martin crouched behind a rock so he could not be seen.

A small group of little shapes straggled out of the opening. They were sighing, and, Martin realized, sobbing. He stuck his head out to get a closer look and gasped.

He saw six children, all very young and thin. Their wrists were tied together in front of them, and their eyes were covered by a thick band of leather tied in back. They wore goose-feather cloaks and they were barefoot. Their wrists were connected to belts, also tied in back, so there was no way the children could take the covering from their eyes. Martin was horrified. If this was the way the Whale People treated captives, what had they done to Tana?

© 1996 Julia Sadowski

The children knelt in a circle and began to dig, scraping at the sand with their tiny fingers. Martin, realizing they could not see, approached them. The biggest child, a boy not more than six, lifted his head.

"Oh, no!" the boy cried. "There is a stranger here!"

Martin knelt down in front of him. "I won't hurt you," he said. "Why are your eyes bound? What are you doing?"

"We're trying to find clams and shellfish to eat because we're so hungry. We're Scanna's slaves," the boy said. "Scanna is king of the Whale People and he doesn't want us to see."

"Why not?" Martin asked.

"Because we would run away. Scanna captured us from our families who live above ground. If we weren't tied up like this, we'd go home."

Martin took his dagger and cut the child's wrist binding. Then he untied the covering over the little boy's eyes. The boy screamed and put his hands to his head.

"The light hurts!" he cried.

"You'll get used to it," Martin said. "Then your eyes will be fine."

Martin untied the wrists of the other five children and removed their eye bandages. He sat with them until they were able to take their hands away from their eyes. He knew every minute he waited might keep him from finding Tana but he knew he had to save these children.

As they waited, they told him the tunnel they had come from led straight to Scanna's underground cave.

"Does he have a new older slave, a young woman?" Martin asked.

"Yes, but he does not treat her like a slave. He gives her plenty of food," said one of the boys.

"But she's sad" added one of the girls. "She cries all the time."

In a couple of hours, they did not see well but they could see shapes.

"Now we can find our way home!" the boy cried.

"How will you get there?" Martin asked. The children pointed to another entrance they said led up through the earth to a cliff over the beach.

"I could get Tana out that way," he said. "Thanks for telling me."

"Thank you and good luck!" the boy said as he led the others into the tunnel that would take them home.

Martin entered the tunnel that led to Scanna's kingdom. The only light came from glimmering eels in the streams flowing along the floor. Martin walked close to the walls, not wanting to slip and fall. He came to a second cave with deep tide pools filled with the wonderful colors of sea anemones. Martin stopped and looked at them.

Sea anemones do not grow in very cold water, he thought. Not only that, but I'm not cold either.

He put his hand in the water. It was as warm as the sea back home. But he knew he was under an ice-covered ice river in the coldest part of the northern sea. There must be a warm underground river that feeds these caves, he thought. No wonder the Whale People picked this place to live. The tunnel led to a second cave that had a single exit that led to a third cave. Martin saw torchlight so he huddled against the wall.

Three giant men were sitting on the ground inside the cave arguing loudly. Martin gasped. They were much larger than he was and he was no match for all three of them. He listened.

"Scanna will kill us if we don't go back with some firewood," the largest of the three said.

"We can't chop wood with this axe. It has a broken handle," the middle-sized man replied.

"We have no way to carve a new handle or fix the old handle. We have no wood here and no way to carve the old one until it fits into the blade," the third man added.

"One of us must tell Scanna we broke the axe, so he will give us another one," the first man suggested.

"Scanna will kill whoever tells him the axe is broken," commented the second man.

Martin looked down at his sharp dagger and stepped into the cave.

"I can fix your axe," he said.

The three men jumped to their feet.

"Who are you?" cried the first.

"You can't come here!" cried the second.

"We are ordered to kill all strangers!" shouted the third.

Martin gulped and said: "But I can fix your axe. Look."

He showed them his dagger.

The biggest man roared with laughter.

"What a stupid boy!" he cried. "We can steal your dagger; then use it to carve an axe and kill you anyway."

Martin, thinking fast, said: "No, you can't."

"Why not?" demanded the second man.

"Because my dagger is magic and can work only for me."
The second man said "Huh!" and grabbed the dagger.
Martin twisted the dagger it cut the man's hand.
"Ow!" the man yelped, letting go.
"See." Martin said.
The men looked at each other.
   "Aw, come on," the biggest man said, after a couple of seconds. "We don't owe Scanna anything. Let this guy carve us a handle."

The others relaxed. Martin took the old axe blade and quickly cut out the old piece of broken handle. Then he took the leftover piece of the old handle and shaped it to fit the old blade.

"Hey, he's good," the big man said.

"What brings you to this dreadful place?" asked the middle-sized man.

"Scanna kidnapped my wife, Tana, and my life isn't worth anything without her," Martin told them.

The three men nodded.

"Is she that that one with the white hair?" the biggest man asked.

"You saw her? She's all right?" Martin cried. His heart thumped with joy.

"Scanna's got her all right," the middle-sized one said. "And he has not hurt her. He is marrying her tonight."

"But she's already my wife!" Martin cried.

"Scanna doesn't care about that," said the third man.

Martin said. "Please help me. I have to get her back!"

The three nodded.

"We'll say that we never saw you," the biggest man said. "We were out getting wood when you came in."

The middle-sized man pointed to a tunnel behind them and said: "You go right through there, and it will lead you to the big chamber. You better hurry. The ceremony is set for this afternoon."

"What happens at the ceremony?" Martin asked.

"Scanna's priests pour sea water over the bride to bind her to the undersea world while Scanna looks on, his magical fin representing the fire of the underground sun."

"What magical fin?"

"It is the color of copper and blinds any human who looks at it directly. So if you grab your wife, don't look back. You will be blinded by the helmet and they'll catch up to you."

"I won't," Martin said.

"Oh, and there's one thing that might help you," the biggest man said.

"What's that?"

"The slime."

"The slime?"

"The Whale People cover themselves with green sea slime for ceremonies. Their hands are slick. And you are already covered with some kind of grease."

"Mountain goat fat," Martin said

"Ah. Good stuff," the smallest man said.

Martin nodded.

"Thanks," he said. He pointed to the tunnel "Through there?" he asked.

"Yup. We gotta go now," the biggest man said. "We have to get driftwood for the fires."

Martin watched as the three men headed down the tunnel away from him.

Martin climbed into the tunnel they had pointed out. It was dark and muddy and it led downward over barnacle-covered steps. He could see a brilliant light ahead of him and kept going until he came to the opening to a massive cave that was a bright as day. Martin hid in the niche beside the entrance looked down. The cave rose in tiers as high as he could see. It was so big that houses had been built on several of the levels. His tunnel's entrance was on the second level. Steps from the entrance led to a walkway around the cave to the back of a raised platform on which stood two black thrones. Other steps led down the front of the platform where hundreds of human-like beings dressed in green fish scales and draped with dark seaweed were gathering.

Then to his horror, Martin saw Tana, her eyes were covered by a band of gold fabric, walk onto the platform and take her seat on one of the thrones. She looked pale and frightened. She was followed by four blind-folded servants carrying flaming torches. Two of the torch-bearers took their places on each side of the thrones.

Rays of light shot from a shape rising from behind the thrones. Martin remembered the man's warning and did not look at the light but at the floor of the cave.

The Whale People threw themselves onto their stomachs with their eyes covered by their hands. Martin watched the shadow cast by the Whale King as Scanna took his place on the throne beside Tana.

Martin knew he had to get her away immediately. But how? He heard footsteps behind him so he ducked into a niche beside the entrance as a procession of priests, dressed in green robes, carrying jugs of water on their heads, walked past him. They headed down to the floor, around the edge of the giant cavern and up the steps behind the platform where they lined up behind Scanna.

As one of the last water-bearers passed, Martin reached out from his hiding place, grabbed the priest, knocked him out with a quick blow to the throat and pulled him into the niche. There, Martin slipped into the green robe, tied the blindfold loosely over his own eyes and put the water jug on his own head. The jug spilled its water during the scuffle but because they were blindfolded the other priests did not see Martin join their ranks as the last in the procession. He followed the feet of the man in front of him until he reached the platform behind Scanna.

Martin slipped between the others until he was in the front row. Then, Martin grabbed the water jug from the closest priest and threw its contents on the torch closest to the whale king. Steam puffed and hissed all over Scanna's copper helmet and created a thick, gray cloud.

The priests screamed and ran down the steps behind the platform. Scanna roared. Martin tore off his blindfold, ducked around the throne and grabbed Tana. The frightened priests were blocking the way he came so Martin dragged Tana down the steps in front and pulled her through the crowd for the moment still face-down on the ground.

As it was, Martin and Tana got halfway across the floor before green hands and scaly arms tried to stop them. Luckily, the wood chopper had been right, Scanna's people were covered with slime so Tana and Martin were able to slither and wriggle their way free toward the tunnel opening. As they approached the steps, the closest Whale People had removed their blindfolds and tried to grab the pair but Tana and Martin slipped away as if they had been buttered.

They were almost at the exit when Martin felt heat searing the back of his head. The light behind him turned the walls to diamonds. He felt Tana stumble. He knew she could not look back, must not look back or she would be lost forever.

Squeezing his eyelids shut, he turned his head toward her, and without opening his eyes, pulled her around in front of him. He covered her eyes with his other hand as he pushed her ahead of him out of the cavern and down the tunnel.

Behind them, the crowd screamed in pain. Scanna's blinding blast had been intended to target Martin and Tana. Instead, it blinded many of his own people.

Tana and Martin did not stop running until they came to the tunnel the goose-feather children had used to go home. They ran through it until they were high on a cliff under a cold, bright-blue sky. Martin looked down at Tana.

"Can you still see? You didn't look back did you?" he asked.

"I almost did," she said. "But I remembered that when someone looks back as they run usually falls, so I stopped myself. It's always better to look forward"

Martin smiled at her. Her eyes were as clear as the sea below them. But where her cheek had turned toward Scanna's light, it had been burned. A mark in the shape of a killer whale fin would remain on her face for as long as she lived.

Martin kissed the mark and led Tana down to the shore. The warm sun drove away the fog and brought them to the beach where the old cedar stood and where Swallow and Marmot waited anxiously.

Tana and Martin lived happily together for the rest of their lives. They had seven children, three boys and four girls. All had white hair and gray eyes but all the girls bore the magical fin shape on their cheeks.

Once in a while, particularly at sunset, they thought they saw a bright copper fin brightening the waves far out on the horizon. Tana never walked alone in the sea again. But Tana knew Scanna of the dark world under the sea would never be able to capture her as long as Martin was there to hold her fast and as long as they stayed in lands ruled by the sun.

Credit: Barbeau, Marius, 1950. *Totem Poles: According to Crests and Topics*. A Haida house post of Massett, showing man and wife holding on to the killer whale.

Through the Doorway...

The fires in have burned low, and the children are in their sleeping quarters of soft bark and fur. The carved cedar boxes have been put away, and the wooden spoons have been polished and put aside.

Dark night has fallen on the ancient Haida. They have gone to live in the land of their dreams, through the doorway, through the totem, and into the spirit world of silver creeks and gentle creatures, where all things live in peace.

Sources and References

Note to e-version readers: *Copy and paste links into the browser of your choice. It will not always work on a click.*

1. Barbeau Marius, *Haida Myths Illustrated by Argillite Carvings,* Bulletin No. 127, Anthropological Series No. 32.The book was printed by Ministry of Resources and Development, Department of Resources and Development, National Parks Branch, National Museum of Canada in 1953. Marius Barbeau was among the first anthropologists to notice the similarities between fables from the Northwest Indian culture and the Homeric tradition around the world.

2. Barbeau, Marius. 1950. *Totem Poles: According to Crests and Topics*. Vol. 1. Ottawa: Dept. of Resources and Development, National Museum of Canada. (National Museum of Canada bulletin; 119-Vol. I)**.** Museum of Anthropology, University of British Columbia.

3. Chief Henry Speck, Kwakiutl artist known as Chief Ozistalis of the Tla-Wis-Tsis of Turnour Island; and other talented Haida artists the author met while researching a series of articles on Northwest Indian art for *The Montreal Star* in 1964.

4. Geological Survey of Canada Collection, Tribes _ Haida "Skedans Indian village, Haida tribe. Louise Island, Queen Charlotte Islands, British Columbia, Canada, July 18th, 1878, photographed by G.M. Dawson, Library and Archives Canada, accession number 1969-120, negative 248, reproduction copy number PA 37754

Website references:

http://www.civilization.ca/cmc/exhibitions/tresors/barbeau/mbp0503e.shtml

http://www.civilization.ca/research-and-collections/library-and-archives/library-collections/

http://www.historymuseum.ca/cmc/exhibitions/aborig/haida/haindexe.shtml

http://www.civilization.ca/research-and-collections/library-and-archives/rights-and-permissions/

http://www.akhistorycourse.org/articles/article.php?artID=194

http://www.pc.gc.ca/eng/pn-np/bc/gwaiihaanas/natcul/natcul3.aspx

http://en.wikipedia.org/wiki/Haida_Gwaii#mw-navigation

http://catalogue.civilization.ca/musvw/List.csp?Profile=LibraryOnly&OpacLanguage=eng&SearchMethod=Find_1&PageType=Start&PreviousList=Start&NumberToRetrieve=10&RecordNumber=&WebPageNr=1&StartValue=1&Database=1_CMC1&Index1=1*Keywordsbib&EncodedRequest=*CF*04*15*8B*11*1A*3D*E0*F6*87*10ya*1A*81*DA&WebAction=NewSearch&SearchT1=totem poles&SearchTerm1=totem poles&OutsideLink=Yes

http://www.civilization.ca/cmc/exhibitions/tresors/barbeau/mbp0502e.shtml

http://www.civilization.ca/cmc/exhibitions/tresors/barbeau/mbp0502e.shtml

http://www.historymuseum.ca/cmc/exhibitions/tresors/barbeau/mbh0100e.shtml

http://www.pc.gc.ca/eng/pn-np/bc/gwaiihaanas/natcul/natcul3.aspx

Notes from websites

Marius Barbeau Biography

Marius Barbeau was among the first anthropologists to notice similarities between fables from the Northwest Indian culture and the Homeric tradition around the world.

A pioneer in the fields of anthropology and folk culture, Marius Barbeau's (1883-1969) work won international acclaim. He was a three-time award winner of Québec's prestigious Prix David, the recipient of honorary doctorates from the Universities of Montréal and Oxford, and was named a Companion of the Order of Canada. In 1985 Marius Barbeau was recognized as a "person of national historic importance" by the Historic Sites and Monuments Board of Canada, and a plaque, making official this designation, was unveiled in 1990 in the Salon Marius Barbeau in the Canadian Museum of Civilization. In addition, the highest point in the Canadian Arctic, a mountain on Ellesmere Island, was given the name "Barbeau Peak", in his honor.

Marius Barbeau was born on March 5, 1883 in Sainte-Marie de Beauce, Québec, Canada. He obtained a law degree from Université Laval, and went on to win a Rhodes scholarship to Oxford University, where he obtained a degree in Anthropology. In 1911, as an anthropologist, Barbeau joined the National Museum, (at that time part of the Geological Survey of Canada) and worked there until his retirement in 1949. He remained closely associated with the Museum until his death.

Barbeau's first research interest was the Native peoples of Eastern Canada, especially the Huron. His research in the field of Native studies soon grew to include work on the songs, customs, legends, art and social organization of Native cultures in the Western and Prairie regions.

Next he turned to French Canada, popularizing the distinctive songs, folk legends and popular and traditional art through numerous books and articles. His interest in Native and French Canadian art led Barbeau to work with such artists as A.Y. Jackson, Emily Carr and Ernest MacMillan. Whatever his research, Barbeau remained an inveterate collector - from French Canada some 400 folk tales and 7,000 songs were collected, along with 2,000 artifacts from across Canada. His writings total over 1,000 books and articles.

BARBEAU, Marius. 1950. Totem Poles: According to Crests and Topics. Vol. 1. Ottawa: Dept. of Resources and Development, National Museum of Canada. 433 . (National Museum of Canada bulletin; 119-Vol. I).*The paper version is out of print. Available in English only*
http://www.historymuseum.ca/cmc/exhibitions/tresors/barbeau/mbp0509e.shtml

Gwaii Haanas National Park Reserve, National Marine Conservation Area Reserve, and Haida Heritage Site

The Canadian government and the Council of the Haida Nation manage the Gwaii Haanas. The name means "Islands of Beauty" in the Haida language and embodies the rugged beauty and rich ecology of this remote Pacific Coastal region.

The Haida Gwaii Watchmen work closely with Parks Canada to watch over important cultural sites including the standing poles at SGang Gwaay, a UNESCO World Heritage Site.

****

Archaeological evidence of human habitation on these islands dates back over 12,500 years and generations of Haida have been and still are nourished by the rich abundance of Haida Gwaii. The Haida developed a complex society on these "Islands of Beauty" thanks to readily accessible food and resources like the cedar tree. Haida artist, Bill Reid, describes its significance:

> *Oh, the cedar tree!*
> *If mankind in its infancy*
> *had prayed for the perfect substance*
> *for all materials and aesthetic needs,*
> *an indulgent god could have provided*
> *nothing better.*

—From Out of the Silence (1971) by Bill Reid

Both red and yellow cedars are used for a variety of purposes: the bark is woven into clothing and baskets, and the wood is used for masks, bentwood boxes, houses and monumental poles and the ingeniously designed Haida dug-out canoe. In the Haida worldview, everything is connected to everything else.

Yahguudang is the Haida word that encompasses the idea of "Respect for all living things." Copper was the ultimate symbol of wealth among the Haida and is associated with Copper Woman of Haida myth. Throughout the coast, shields made of copper were exchanged at ever higher values between chiefs at potlatch feasts.

Among the Kwakwaka'wakw (or Kwakiutl) to the south of Haida Gwaii, coppers were particularly associated with the distribution of wealth at wedding feasts. The Haida used coppers as a marker and symbol of wealth, and some wealthy chiefs owned a dozen or more.

****

Haida Gwaii

Major islands: Graham Island, Moresby Island
Area: 10,180 km2 (3,931 sq mi)
Highest elevation: 1,164 m (3,819 ft)
Highest point
Province: British Columbia

Haida Gwaii (Haida: X̱aayda gwaay /ˈhaɪdə gwaɪ/, HY-duh-GWY, literally "Islands of the [Haida] People"),[3] also known as the Queen Charlotte Islands and the Charlottes, is an archipelago on the North Coast of British Columbia, Canada, populated mostly by Haida people. Haida Gwaii consists of two main islands: Graham Island in the north and Moresby Island in the south, along with approximately 150 smaller islands with a total landmass of 10,180 km2 (3,931 sq mi). Other major islands include Anthony, Langara, Louise, Lyell, Burnaby, and Kunghit Islands.

The islands are separated from the British Columbia mainland to the east by Hecate Strait. Vancouver Island lies to the south, across Queen Charlotte Sound, while the U.S. state of Alaska is to the north, across the disputed Dixon Entrance.

Some of the islands are protected under federal legislation as Gwaii Haanas National Park Reserve and Haida Heritage Site, which is mostly Moresby Island (Gwaii Haanas in Haida) and adjoining islands and islets.

On June 3, 2010, the Haida Gwaii Reconciliation Act officially renamed the islands Haida Gwaii as part of a reconciliation protocol between British Columbia and the Haida people.

... At the time of colonial contact, the population was roughly 10,000 people, residing in several towns and including slave populations drawn from other clans of Haida as well as other tribes. It is estimated that ninety percent of the population died during the 1800s from smallpox; other diseases arrived as well, including typhoid, measles, and syphilis, affecting many more inhabitants.

By 1900, only 350 people remained. Towns were abandoned as people left their homes for the towns of Skidegate and Masset, cannery towns on the mainland, or for Vancouver Island. Today, only some 3,800 people live on the islands. About 70% of the indigenous people (Haida) live in two communities at Skidegate and Old Masset, with a population of about 700 each. In total the Haida make up 45% of the population of the islands.

Anthony Island and the island of Ninstints were made a UNESCO World Heritage Site in 2006; in the decision, the decline in population wrought by disease was referenced when citing the 'vanished civilization' of the Haida.[6]

****

Early History

The Haida are a linguistically distinct group and they have a complex class and rank system consisting of two main clans: Eagles and Ravens.

The west coast of North America likely saw the first sustained arrival of people to the continent. Although there are other theories, most scientists believe that the first significant groups of people came from Asia, through today's Bering Strait area, then through modern Alaska, and from there spread throughout North America and to South America.

Links and diversity within the Haida Nation was gained through a cross lineal marriage system between the clans. This system was also important for the transfer of wealth within the Nation, with each clan reliant on the other for the building of longhouses, the carving of totem poles and other items of cultural importance.

Noted seafarers, the Haida occupied more than 100 villages throughout the Islands. Like the New Zealand Maori the Haida were skilled traders, with established trade links with their neighboring First Nations on the mainland and farther afield. The Haida had a stable existence and vibrant culture at the time of European contact.

****

Northwest Coast Culture

The Eyak, Tlingit, Haida and Tsimshian share a common and similar Northwest Coast Culture with important differences in language and clan system. Anthropologists use the term "Northwest Coast Culture" to define the Eyak, Tlingit, Haida and Tsimshian cultures, as well as that of other peoples indigenous to the Pacific coast, extending as far as northern Oregon.

...The Haida people speak an isolate (unrelated to other) language, Haida, with three dialects: Skidegate and Masset in British Columbia, Canada and the Kaigani dialect of Alaska

...The original homeland of the Haida people is the Queen Charlotte Islands in British Columbia, Canada. Prior to contact with Europeans, a group migrated north to the Prince of Wales Island area within Alaska. This group is known as the "Kaigani" or Alaska Haidas. Today, the Kaigani Haida live mainly in two villages, Kasaan and the consolidated village of Hydaburg.

...During the past few decades, several New World archaeological sites have been claimed to date to the period of the last ice age. The earliest widespread occupation that is universally accepted by archaeologists, however, begins only 12, 000 years ago.

****

Haida Cultural Sites

K'uuna Llnagaay (Skedans)
T'aanuu Llnagaay (Tanu)
Hlk'yah GaawGa (Windy Bay)
Gandll K'in Gwaay.yaay (Hotspring Island)
SGang Gwaay Llnagaay (Anthony Island)

SGang Gwaay Llnagaay © Parks Canada / J. Brown

SGang Gwaay (Anthony Island) is located in the exposed southwest corner of Gwaii Haanas. The Haida name means Wailing Island, based on a sound created at certain tides when air is pushed through a hole in a rock on the island. This sound is thought to resemble the keening of a woman. SGang Gwaay consists of a larger island and 27 small islets.

The village, SGang Gwaay Llnagaay, is a UNESCO World Heritage Site and is located in a sheltered bay on the east side of the island. Visitors can explore upright and fallen poles, house pits, and standing posts and beams of longhouses.

Monumental Poles

Poles carved with crests of the Eagle and Raven clans of the Haida are found at SGang Gwaay Llnagaay (formerly known as Ninstints), a UNESCO World Heritage Site on Anthony Island, and at the Haida Heritage Site of K'uuna Llnagaay (Skedans).

Haida Longhouses

Longhouses, the remnants of which can be seen at T'aanuu Llnagaay (Tanu), K'uuna Llnagaay (Skedans), and SGang Gwaay, were constructed in an uniquely Haida way. With amazingly large posts and beams defining the enormous tiered house pits, longhouse remains offer a window into the historic Haida way of life.

Haida Gwaii Watchmen cabins, hotsprings, culturally modified trees and more can be seen in Gwaii Haanas. Cultural sites are also found in rivers, on beaches, in the intertidal zone and in the forest.

Totem Bight State Historical Park

Credit: Totem Bight State Park, Ketchikan; The Clan House

http://dnr.alaska.gov/parks/units/totembgh.htm Alaska's Incredible Totem Poles (part II)
2009.08.16

http://www.photoblog.com/lifeisgood/2009/08/16/alaskas-incredible-totem-poles-part-ii.html

The Story of Totem Bight

With the growth of non-Native settlements in Southeast Alaska in the early 1900's, and the decline of a barter economy, Natives moved to communities where work was available. The villages and totem poles they left behind were soon overgrown by forests and eroded by weather. In 1938 the U.S. Forest Services began a program aimed at salvaging and reconstructing these large cedar monuments.

By using Civilian Conservation Corps (CCC) funds to hire skilled carvers from among the older Natives, two things took place: young artisans learned the art of carving totem poles, and totems which had been left to rot in the woods were either repaired or duplicated.

Alaskan architect Linn Forrest supervised construction of the model Native village for this site, then called Mud Bight. The fragments of old poles were laid beside freshly cut cedar logs, and every attempt was made to copy them traditionally. Tools for carving were hand-made, modeled on the older tools used before coming of Europeans. Samples of Native paints were created from natural substances such as clam shells, lichen, graphite, copper pebbles, and salmon eggs; natural colors were then duplicated with modern paints.

By the time World War II slowed down the CCC project, the community house and 15 poles were in place. The name of the site was then changed to Totem Bight. At statehood, in 1959, title to the land passed from the federal government to the State of Alaska, and the site was added to the National Register of Historic Places in 1970. At that time it came under the management of the State's Department of Natural Resources for continuing historic preservation treatment by the Division of Parks and Outdoor Recreation.

http://dnr.alaska.gov/parks/units/totembgh.htm

The Clan House

A community house or clan house of this size could have housed 30 to 50 people.

Inside is one large room with a central fireplace surrounded by a planked platform. The walls and floors were hand-adzed to smooth the surface and remove splinters. The dwelling served as living quarters for several families of a particular lineage. Each was allotted its own space but shared a common fire.

Housewares, treasured items, and blankets were stored under the removable floor boards, and food items were hung from the beams and rafters. The members belonging to the house would be headed by a house chief of the same lineage.

The carved house posts supporting the beams inside symbolize the exploits of Duk-toothl. He is a man of Raven phratry wearing \ a weasel skin hat who showed his strength by tearing a sea lion in two. The painting on the house front was designed by Charles Brown. It is a stylized Raven with each eye elaborated into a face. Designs on the house fronts were rare, and occurred only in cases of great wealth.

On the front corner posts sits a man in a spruce root hat with the crest design on his face and cane in hand. He is ready for a dance or potlatch.

http://www.pc.gc.ca/eng/pn-np/bc/gwaiihaanas/index.aspx

Post Contact History

Skedans Village circa 1878 © G.M. Dawson / Library and Archives Canada

Survivor migration

In the late 1700s, during the time of first contact with "those from away" at least 20,000 Haida are estimated to have lived on the islands. The population plummeted with the introduction of diseases such as smallpox, measles and tuberculosis. By the late 1800s, fewer than 600 Haida were left on Haida Gwaii.

...The maritime fur trade around Haida Gwaii occurred largely between 1787 and 1840. The large-scale trade in pelts hunted by the Haida over this period devastated the sea otter population and precipitated enormous cultural changes for the Haida.

The traders' (mostly British and American) goods were in demand by the Haida, as much as the furs were in demand by faraway markets.

A great amount of wealth was gained during this period by all involved. Trading ship's records indicate that more than 100 pelts a day were collected from some villages during the peak periods.

The sea otter was so important to the Haida and the islands ecosystems that the Archipelago Management Board (the co-operative board which manages Gwaii Haanas National Park Reserve, National Marine Conservation Area Reserve and Haida Heritage Site) chose that as their crest.

First Nations Art of the Pacific Northwest Coast

Volcano Woman

Text from:
http://www.spiritwrestler.com/catalog/index.php

Volcano Woman is perhaps one of the oldest and most revered legends which tells of a mortal's fate if he/she does not treat sacred objects or creatures with respect. In defense of her beloved wild creatures, she controls the powerful volcanoes. Stories tell of how the killing of a frog leads the Volcano woman to destroy an entire village.

Volcano Woman is a supernatural, powerful person in First Nations mythology. She had a son who, like his mother, had supernatural abilities. He often liked to change from his Human form to that of a Frog (Wukus).

Years ago, a Prince and his two friends went fishing. Hungry, they lay their food on leaves. The Wukus (Frog), being mischievous, jumped on their food. Twice the young Prince threw the Frog into the shrubs but on the third time they threw the frog into the fire and killed the innocent creature.

A few nights later, a woman could be heard crying and wailing. "Who has done this, come forward and I will spare your village." This warning went unheeded for some time until finally a Woman of the Elders went to the village outskirts to see her. Volcano Woman instructed the Woman of the Elders to send forth the three young men and she would spare the village from volcanic destruction. The Woman of the Elders begging for the sake of the Village told of Volcano Woman's ultimatum - but this warning went unheeded.

On the final night of the village's existence, Volcano Woman was heard saying, "I asked for those responsible to take heed and now you will know my vengeance." The Village shook, a Volcano erupted, destroying the village and all who lived there.

www.ingramcontent.com/pod-product-compliance
Lightning Source LLC
Chambersburg PA
CBHW041409010726
47507CB00001B/49